A letter for Emma.

A letter for Emma.

Mollie Thompson

Scripture Union
130 City Road, London EC1V 2NJ

By the same author

The Island Girl

© Mollie Thompson 1989
First published 1989

ISBN 0 86201 569 3

Phototypeset by Input Typesetting Ltd., London
Printed and bound in Great Britain by Cox and Wyman
Ltd., Reading

1

The ping-pong ball went sailing through the air, hit the wall and bounced.

'Where did it go?' Emma called to her partner.

'Over there somewhere but I can't see it,' Lauren replied.

The two girls looked in corners and under furniture but it seemed to have vanished.

'Never mind, it had a tiny crack in it anyway,' said Emma, 'so it's no great loss.'

Emma stretched out on the thick white rug with her hands behind her head. It was her favourite position because, as she said, there is never enough room in chairs for people with long legs. With her jeans she was wearing a blue jumper with a cowl neck, and after playing table tennis most of the morning she felt very hot. She pushed her hair away from her face. Her hair was the same colour as her mother's, a rich auburn, and she had such fair skin that each summer brought a fresh crop of freckles, much to Emma's disgust. In contrast Lauren was dark-haired and her skin always tanned to a beautiful golden brown.

There were several other rugs scattered about on the polished floor of the games room, and some cane tables and chairs near where Lauren was sitting flicking through the pages of a magazine.

'Didn't Anita say she was coming?' asked Lauren, glancing at her watch.

'Yes, she said she was bringing her tapes, too. I hope she remembers.'

Just then through the open window they heard the click of the latch as the side gate opened and Anita appeared round the end of the building wheeling her bicycle. Emma jumped up and ran across to open the garden door for her.

'Yes, I've brought them,' Anita said in answer to Emma's questioning look.

'Lauren has worked out this new dance routine. It's great,' Emma said enthusiastically.

'It'll be even better with music,' Lauren grinned.

Emma slotted the cassette into the tape deck and pressed the play button while Anita moved scatter rugs out of Lauren's way.

'Now, watch this,' said Emma as Lauren began talking them through the movements as she danced.

'One, two, turn and dip. Right foot cross and arms up.' She repeated it over and over again as Emma and Anita watched.

'Come on,' Lauren called out above the sound of the music, 'count it to eight beats in your head.'

Soon Emma and Anita were chanting in unison as they danced . . . one, two, three and four. Five and six, seven, eight . . . The tape ended, was rewound and they started again but they listened to the singer instead of counting. When they stopped for a rest Emma said, 'If we worked at it we could get it perfect before the Youth Club disco.'

'Could we teach it to some of the others?' Anita asked.

'Yes, we could, but for now let's stick to three of us and get it right,' Lauren said. 'Are you ready for another go?'

The others nodded and they started again, turning the volume up higher until the sound throbbed back from the walls and ceiling. Finally they decided that they'd done enough practice for one day. Emma flopped down on her favourite rug and while Lauren sorted through the collection of tapes, Anita sank down into the body-hugging depths of a bean bag.

'You are lucky, you know,' she said.

'How so?' Emma asked.

'Having a place like this for your own where nobody comes and says, "Turn that noise down".'

'I suppose I am. I can do almost anything I like in my playroom. Paul calls it the games room which sounds much too important, I think. When he comes home from boarding school he plays billiards mostly.'

Anita looked around but could see no billiard table.

'It's a folding table and we put it in the broom cupboard when it's not in use.'

'I like this one, don't you?' Lauren said, putting in another tape.

The three girls were at the far end of the room and didn't see the door into the house slowly opening. Sarah, Emma's mother, stood quietly watching them and then she flicked the light switch on and off several times. That soon attracted the girls' attention and Emma looked up with a smile.

'Hello, Mum, I didn't hear you come in.'

'I'm not surprised. I doubt if you'd have heard even if I'd backed the car in through the window,' she called holding her hands over her ears and pulling a face.

'Sorry, is it too loud?' Emma reached across and turned the machine off.

'Not that it was disturbing me, in fact I couldn't hear it at the front of the house but when I came down the passage it hit me like a . . .'

7

'Brick,' suggested Emma. Her mother nodded.

'Sometimes I do wonder what your hearing will be like in a few years' time: not just you three, I mean the disco generation.'

'Does it really affect our ears?' Lauren asked, looking horrified.

'Yes, it might do. So do you think you could manage with just a little less volume perhaps?'

'If you put it like that, yes, I suppose it's not worth making ourselves deaf,' Anita said, looking very thoughtful.

'However,' continued Sarah, 'I didn't come here to deliver a lecture but to give you this, Emma.'

Sarah handed her daughter a large sheet of paper which had been folded into three and sealed with a blob of scarlet sealing wax. Emma's eyes opened wide with amazement.

'What's this?' she asked, picking at the red blob with her finger.

Her mother smiled. 'Years ago people used to seal important documents like that; melting the wax onto the paper and pressing a seal into the wax while it was still warm.'

Lauren and Anita both touched the surface of the sealing wax and could feel the indentation left by the seal.

'Look, it's some sort of bird,' said Lauren.

'Where's this come from? Is it for me?' Emma asked eventually.

'Yes, it's for you, it's from your great-grandmother in Malaysia. And you're right about the bird, Lauren; it's a heron and that was Great-Grandma's maiden name.'

'Well, open it then,' Anita urged.

Emma looked at her two friends. Then she closed her eyes and put on a haughty expression. 'I suppose I might allow you to see my important document.'

Prising the sealing wax off the paper she opened the letter and read the message in its beautiful flowing handwriting:

> *My dear Emma,*
> *How strange it is to be writing to my namesake, my*
> *great-granddaughter whom I have never met.*
> *Happily that situation will soon be altered. I have*
> *your photograph on my desk as I write and I see*
> *that you have your mother's chestnut hair, as have*
> *all our family. Apart from that I know very little*
> *about you except that you are now eleven years old.*
> *How time flies. I am looking forward so much to*
> *meeting you, and to being with my family-in-England*
> *after all these years away.*
>   *God bless you and keep you,*
>   *from Emma*
>   *Your loving Great-Grandmother.*

Emma looked up at her mother and then down at the letter again.

'It's a nice letter, but it sounds odd . . . the way the words are put.'

'That's probably because people used to write differently when your great-grandma went to school many years ago. Fashions alter, you know.'

'I didn't know we had the same name. She's your dad's mother, isn't she?'

'That's right, and she'll be leaving the rubber plantation in Malaysia and coming to live here soon. There are a lot more details in her letter to me but I'll tell you about that later.'

'Wow, how exciting,' gasped Anita, 'having a great-grandmother from foreign parts.'

'I like that bit with the sealing wax. It's sort of exotic and different. I wonder what the old lady is like?' Lauren said.

'I'll leave you now then, I've still got some things to do,' Sarah said, moving towards the door. Then looking back over her shoulder she added, 'I've made some iced buns; they're cooling on a wire tray in the kitchen if you're interested.'

'Thanks, Mum,' Emma said, following her mother out of the playroom.

When she returned with a plate of iced buns and three coffee mugs the girls settled down to their snack with enthusiasm.

'My Nana and Gramps live on the Isle of Man. We often go over and visit them in the summer,' Lauren said, reaching to put her coffee mug back on the tray. 'Have you ever been over to the island?' The girls shook their heads.

'It's lovely there. Nana once took me to a farm where they look after retired horses. There were still horse-drawn trams along the sea front and when the horses get too old to work they live the rest of their lives on this farm.'

'Oh, that's lovely; a sort of retirement home,' Anita said.

'Right. And once they get there they don't seem to be half as old; they gallop round the fields kicking their heels in the air, happy to be free.'

'What about *your* grandparents?' asked Emma, looking across at Anita.

'My dad's parents live just outside London. They have a boat moored at a marina somewhere. I remember once they took us across the Channel and we spent the week-end along the French coast. And then there's Grandma Jean, she only lives down the road from us. She has this huge tree in her garden and when the fruit is ripe she makes the most fantastic crab-apple jelly.'

Emma sat listening as Anita and Lauren talked about their grandparents, each remembering interesting and funny things that had happened when they were little. Emma had never known either of her grandparents but as she listened to her friends she began to realise what a lot she must have missed.

Her thoughts were interrupted by Lauren clicking her fingers in front of her face. 'We've been doing all the talking, so what about you?'

'I've a hazy memory of Grandma York, she was Dad's mother, but I was only a toddler then. Mum's parents died in an air crash long before I was born; so really there isn't much to say.'

'But that's all changed now, hasn't it,' Anita said cheerfully, 'because soon you'll have the sealing wax lady, all the way from Malaysia.'

At the end of the morning, after Anita and Lauren had gone home, Emma wandered into the kitchen and leaned her elbows on the breakfast bar, propping her chin in her hands.

'How old is Great-Grandma?' she asked.

Sarah thought for a moment and then said, 'Somewhere in her early eighties I should think. I haven't seen her since Paul was a baby and that was my last year in Malaysia.'

'I expect she'll need a lot of help now.'

'I expect she will,' said her mother, handing the place mats to Emma.

While she set the table her thoughts ran unchecked and before long in her imagination she could see the whole picture. A frail little old lady with grey hair pulled back in a bun at the back of her neck, wearing a big white pinny and leaning on a walking stick. Emma decided that she was going to be helpful and useful in all sorts of ways: she could dust and clean for Great-Grandma, or do the gardening or go shopping. As her thoughts wove a network of possibilities they also produced a lot of questions that needed answers.

'Mum, tell me some things that you remember about Great-Grandma, and tell me what was in her letter to you.'

'That will have to wait until your dad is home and then we can have a family conference.'

That evening Emma was the first to hear the car coming up the drive, then she heard the garage door slam. Dad was home. As he came in the back way Emma was there waiting for him at the kitchen door.

'Hello, love, and what have you been doing today?'

This was what he always said when he came home. It had grown into a little ritual and she would reply, 'Oh nothing much . . . except . . .' and then she would tell him whatever it was. However, this evening in reply to his question she tried to look as mysterious as possible and said, 'Something . . .'

He raised his eyebrows. 'Something? Tell me about it then.'

'A letter for me. A letter sealed with sealing wax.'

'So what is the letter about?'

Emma shook her head. 'It isn't exactly a secret . . . but I'd better let Mum tell you . . . at the family conference.'

Alan walked across the kitchen, gave Sarah a kiss and then said, 'Have you any idea what this girl of ours is muttering about? Something to do with secrets and sealing wax?'

Sarah laughed, 'Yes, and I suppose the kitchen is as good a place as any other to have a family conference. It's a pity Paul isn't here.'

'As serious as that, is it? Something to do with Paul; has he broken a leg playing rugby or something worse?'

'It's nothing like that, it's something nice,' Emma called back as she ran upstairs to her bedroom to fetch Great-Grandma's letter.

'Today I got a letter,' Sarah began '. . . an envelope from Malaysia, from my grandmother and as well as my letter there was one for Emma too. It was sealed with sealing wax, but she'll tell you about her letter.'

'Oh, I remember the old lady, she was still running a rubber plantation out there, wasn't she?' said Alan.

'Well that's the problem, she's not going to be well enough so she's leaving all that and coming back to England.' Sarah handed the envelope to him and he was reading the letter when Emma came back.

His face had a serious look as he turned the page and read on, then he frowned and looked up at Sarah. 'What a sad business,' he said softly.

'What's sad? Tell me,' Emma said.

Dad hesitated for a moment, glancing at Sarah before answering.

'I think it must be sad to leave a home you've lived in all those years. But look, your great-grandma has sent photos of the house and plantation.'

Emma took the photos and looked intently at each in turn. There were some which were obviously of the jungle with brilliant flowers and hanging creepers, and some of tracks through a clearing with brown-skinned men standing in a little group and children staring self-consciously at the camera. There were several different views of the house, built of wood and painted white with a verandah all around. There was even one of a merry-faced Malay gardener with a rake in his hand, but there were no photos of Great-Grandma herself.

'None of Great-Grandma, I wanted to see what she

was like.'

'That often happens when you're the one with the camera in hand,' Mother said from experience.

Emma passed the photos back and then gave her letter to her dad. It still had the sealing wax attached to one side of the fold and he looked at it carefully. Then he ran a finger across its surface.

'It's a long time since I've seen any of this. Parcels used to be of brown paper, sealing wax and string; not wrapped round with sticky tape like they are today.' He read the letter and smiled as he handed it back.

'That's a very nice letter, and fancy her name being Emma also, I'd forgotten that.' Then he turned back to Sarah. 'Have we any idea how long?'

'You mean how long before she comes to England,' Sarah said with great deliberation. 'No, that could be several months or at least as long as it takes for her to settle her business affairs out there.'

While Mother and Dad talked Emma's mind returned to the thoughts she'd had earlier; of how she was going to help Great-Grandma and spend lots of time with her, perhaps listening to stories about life in Malaysia. But she could only do that if she was living somewhere near enough for Emma to cycle.

'Can I just ask one more question. Will Great-Grandma be living near us?'

'Yes, I'm sure she will. Very near probably,' said her mother, smiling.

2

Emma woke to find something lying across her feet. She wriggled her toes but the weight didn't move.

'Get off, Puddy, you shouldn't be on the bed,' she said sleepily.

At the sound of her voice the little grey kitten began a bubbling purr that became louder as he walked up the bedclothes toward Emma's face.

'Yes, of course I love you but are your feet clean?' She stroked the upturned chin and looked into Puddy's unblinking green eyes. The purring continued louder than before.

Emma got out of bed and ran to the window. There were signs that it had rained heavily during the night, the puddle that lay in the hollow on the flat garage roof looked quite deep, and the tarmac path was black instead of grey. Today was the third Saturday in the month and that date had been ringed in red on her calendar because it was the day of the church outing. At first Rev Timms had booked the mini-coach but so many people had wanted to go that he'd had to change to the larger coach instead.

They were going to Beacon Fell and then through Roundel Woods to the picnic area. Everybody had been looking forward to today and it would be a lovely day out if only the weather stayed fine. Emma looked up at the moist grey sky and said under her breath, 'Oh please don't rain', then she went to the bathroom to get washed, leaving Puddy on the landing busily washing his paws.

A little later as Emma came downstairs the telephone rang.

'Shall I get it?' she called.

'If you would, love,' her mother called back from the dining room.

The call was for her dad so Emma left the phone lying on the hall stand and went into the dining room.

'For you, Dad.'

He left the table and she could hear muted sounds of conversation. Then he laughed and hung up the receiver.

'Typical,' he said, returning to the breakfast table. 'The meeting has been cancelled at short notice. It's a good thing I hadn't already left for the office.'

'Does that mean you can come with us?' Emma said quickly.

'Why, where are you going? Shopping?'

'No, Dad, it's the church outing. Had you forgotten?'

'So it is. Ah, but there'll be no room for me, I didn't book a place. I'll stay here and potter about in the garden if it keeps fine.'

Sarah looked across the table at him and then she said, 'That seems a great pity, Alan, you'd be on your own most of the day. Why don't I give Vera a ring and see if there's a spare seat on the coach?'

Five minutes later she came back from the phone with a big smile on her face. 'Well, that's all settled,' she said triumphantly. 'Vera Timms said we couldn't possibly leave you behind.'

At that moment a shaft of sunlight came flooding in through the window and, as the light touched the cut-glass butter dish, it broke into a vivid arc of rainbow colours shining onto the white table cloth.

16

'Isn't that beautiful,' said Emma. 'I do like rainbows.'

'Yes, rainbows are very special things, they can remind us . . .'

Emma was just going to say 'what about?' but she hadn't time to ask the question because the door bell chimed. It was Lauren.

As she came inside she saw the kitten lying on his back, playing a fighting game with the strap of Emma's shoulder bag.

'I didn't know you'd got a kitten. Isn't he gorgeous,' Lauren said, tickling his little fat tummy.

'We only got him a week ago. His name is Puddy.'

'Pudding, did you say?'

'No, Puddy . . . you know, Puddy Tat,' said Emma.

Lauren wrinkled her nose and groaned at the joke.

It wasn't long before everyone was ready. Sarah had quickly packed another set of sandwiches for Alan whilst he went up to change out of his business suit into something more suitable for a day in the woods. Then together they all walked down Wildings Lane to the corner just in time to see the coach coming up from the village.

'Welcome aboard, everybody,' said Rev Timms.

There were greetings from up and down the coach and several choir members called out, 'Glad you could come, Alan.'

Anita had brought her cousin Dave with her and they had saved the seat in front of them for Emma and Lauren.

'Is everyone here now?' asked Robert Timms. 'Good, and it seems that God has granted us a sunny day too.'

The coach was on its way. They travelled through villages, past fields and farmyards and on toward higher ground. Now the road stretched ahead like a winding ribbon threading its way amongst the sheep dotted hillsides. Ahead of them was a series of tree-covered slopes

17

rising to Beacon Fell in the distance. The coach turned off the metalled road, followed a cart track for about half a mile and then stopped.

'Here we are. This is where you walkers and scramblers get out,' said Vera Timms. Then she turned to an elderly lady sitting at the front of the coach, 'But Mrs Porter wants to say a few words.'

Mrs Porter rose to her feet. 'For anyone who doesn't feel like going mountaineering . . . and I'm one of them,' she said, smiling down at her husband, '. . . we have persuaded our son-in-law to drive us along the river route, haven't we, Ben?'

The driver turned round and waved a hand in agreement. 'Yes, and we'll all meet up again near Roundel picnic area.'

There was a general hustle and bustle as some people moved out of the coach and the remainder settled back into their seats. The coach carefully reversed into a field entrance and then returned the way it had come. Most of the walkers drifted into groups as they set off through the bracken, laughing and talking.

Anita introduced her cousin to Emma's parents and Emma, having heard that Dave was interested in model boats, gave her dad a playful thump on the back.

'Another model-maniac to talk to,' she grinned.

'Cheeky,' her dad said, laughing.

Mother had hurried on ahead to say something to one of her neighbours and Emma, Lauren and Anita joined a little group of their friends from the Youth Club. Everyone was climbing steadily upward toward the summit and the further up they went the less talking they did. Before long the three girls dropped behind the rest of their group.

'This is tough going,' panted Lauren.

'But it'll be worth it when we get there,' puffed Emma.

At last they reached the top and stood together looking at the view spread out below them. They could see for miles in every direction and it seemed like a coloured patchwork of fields in different shades of green, depending on the crop that was growing. Thread-like roads connected the warm sun-patterned villages; trees and church spires pointed skyward and a column of twisting smoke told that someone down there was burning garden rubbish.

'I feel like a giant looking down on toytown,' Anita said dreamily.

'Well you don't look like one: more like a garden gnome I'd say,' Emma chuckled. That brought Anita out of her reverie.

'You are rude; just because I'm plumpish.'

'I only meant because of the bobble hat,' said Emma unconvincingly.

'What are they looking at over there, I wonder?' Lauren was pointing toward the place where the rest of the party had gathered. Then the three girls caught up and were just in time to hear Robert Timms saying '. . . . and they think it stood here, near that flat rock, isn't that right, Mr Taylor?'

Emma nudged her mother's arm and mouthed, 'What did?' Mother put her finger on her lips. Mr Taylor was the local historian and she wanted to hear what he had to say.

'Yes indeed; brushwood and dead trees would have been piled here and covered against the weather until that night in 1588 when the local people put a torch to it and set it ablaze. And so one by one the beacon fires carried the news the length and breadth of the country.'

Emma's eyes suddenly brightened with understanding and she said quite loudly, 'The Armada.'

'Quite right. The fleet with which Philip the Second

of Spain had hoped to conquer our land . . .' continued Mr Taylor warming to his subject '. . . was defeated in the Channel and dispersed by the English vessels under Lord Howard of Effingham.'

'Isn't it strange, I'd never thought of it before but that must be how Beacon Fell got its name,' Lauren said.

Emma looked very thoughtful as she stared at the huge slab of weathered sandstone poking up out of the ground.

'Just ordinary people like us, lighting up their fires, hoping the wood wasn't wet; it makes them seem so much nearer to us, doesn't it?' she said to her mother.

The walk down the far side of Beacon Fell was far less exhausting and in no time they had reached the stile leading into Roundel Woods. They reached it only just in time too, because a bank of cloud had blotted out the sun and suddenly it began to pour with rain. Little groups of people huddled against tree trunks where the leaf cover was thickest, and sheltered from the worst of the downpour. As the rain eased off Anita ventured out from under her tree.

'Come on, it's not too bad,' she called, so the others followed her along the path and on towards the wooden buildings which they could see in the distance. The Information Centre had a covered way between the buildings and soon the whole party took shelter there.

They watched as the sun appeared from behind the cloudbank but the rain was still falling. Within seconds a brilliant rainbow arched across the sky seeming to touch the horizon, and Emma looked up at her mother.

'The second time today,' she laughed. 'What was it you said at breakfast about rainbows being special?'

'I think they're special because they can remind us of a passage in the Bible . . . of a covenant . . .' Mother began, but at that point Dave added his comment.

'Simply water droplets acting like a prism; there's nothing at all mysterious about it,' he said.

'She didn't say it was mysterious, she said it was special,' Anita interrupted '. . . and we don't want all that scientific stuff at the moment, thank you very much,' she said rather fiercely. Anita loved her cousin really but he was two years older and acted as though he knew it all, which she found very irritating at times.

By that time they had reached the picnic area and found that the coach had brought the rest of their party. They had now emerged and were each unpacking their picnic lunch onto the waiting rough wood tables.

For the second time Emma had to wait for an explanation about her rainbow. She smiled at her mother and shrugged her shoulders.

When Sarah noticed Vera was heading towards their table she said, 'Wait until they're sitting down, then you could ask Rev Timms, he'll probably be able to give you the exact quotation.'

Robert was already within earshot and as he settled himself onto the bench seat next to his wife he said, 'So what is it that you want to ask me, Emma?'

'It's about rainbows,' she began, 'Mum said that they've a special meaning in the Bible, something about a covenant.'

Robert smiled at her. 'Do you know what a covenant is?'

'A kind of agreement between people,' Emma said.

'That's right, and in Genesis chapter nine we are told that after the flood God made a covenant with Noah and his family.'

Anita joined in the conversation saying, 'So was a rainbow God's promise not to flood them out again?'

'Yes, so it says. Now let me think of the actual quotation,' he paused for a moment. 'Yes, it goes . . . I set my bow in the cloud, and it shall be a sign of the covenant between me and the earth.'

Emma looked up at the sky where the rainbow had been. 'A bow in the cloud, that's a lovely phrase,' she said softly.

Dave was just about to speak but as he opened his mouth Anita glared at him and muttered, 'Don't start again.'

Robert noticed this and turning to Dave asked, 'Were you going to add something?'

'I was going to say that a rainbow is only the refraction of light through water droplets, isn't it?' he said rather defensively.

'Absolutely right, of course it is. As a scientific fact it is true; however it is also true that rainbows are beautiful.'

'And coming after dark clouds and rain they remind us that there is always the promise of a new beginning,' Vera added.

Lauren began fumbling in her bag and produced a hand mirror.

'Look at this,' she said and turned it over to show the rainbow design on the back. 'The shops are full of things with a rainbow on; belts, purses, note books and pencils.'

'Oh yes, they're the in-thing at the moment,' Anita agreed.

'I find that very hopeful,' said Robert. 'It seems to suggest that our world is ready to make a new beginning and enjoy beautiful things.'

During the walk along the nature trail Emma kept remembering what had been said and it made her feel warm inside. How wonderful it would be if everyone in the world wanted a new beginning. Then all the horrid, ugly and cruel things might be changed and swept away.

It was late afternoon by the time everyone had returned to the coach. Some had been on the nature trail through the woods and others had spent time in the tea rooms and gift shop. Once back in their seats Vera counted heads to make sure nobody was missing and then the coach started on the long return journey. Emma and Lauren were both quite tired and it wasn't long before Lauren's head wobbled sleepily onto her friend's shoulder. Meanwhile Emma carefully opened the little parcel which she'd bought at the gift shop. Inside was a small carved wooden mouse with a leather tail and a badge with a rainbow on it. She hadn't bought them for herself and she didn't know who she'd eventually give them to but she felt sure they'd make a nice present for somebody.

Her parents had the seat in front and although Emma wasn't listening to their conversation she couldn't help overhearing some of it. She heard her own name mentioned several times and then the words Malaya and house prices. Emma smiled to herself as she remembered the letter from Great-Grandma with the blob of sealing wax and she wondered just how long it would be before she met the old lady.

At the corner of Wildings Lane Emma and her parents said goodbye to everyone, thanked the Timms for organising everything and then got out. In the gathering dusk they watched the coach's glowing tail lights disappear over the hill and down towards the village.

'I did enjoy today,' Mother said when they were in the house.

'It was great, I'm glad I came,' said Dad.

'Me too,' agreed Emma.

It wasn't until much later that Emma suddenly said, 'In the coach I heard you both talking. Was it about Great-Grandma buying a house here?'

Alan looked surprised. 'Not exactly, not a house; your mother and I were just discussing possibilities.'

'Yes, today was a golden opportunity for Dad and me to talk things through and see what would be best for all of us.'

Emma looked puzzled. 'If she isn't going to buy a house then where *is* she going to live?'

'We thought it would be a good idea if she lived here with us,' Sarah said and then she quickly piled the supper plates on the tray and went into the kitchen.

Emma stroked the sleeping kitten and watched as the very tip of his tail flicked back and forth. She began wondering how Great-Grandma would like sleeping in the guest bedroom; it was a very small room but it did have a lovely view of the orchard with the bee hives.

'Dad, will it be big enough for Great-Grandma?' said Emma, thinking of the guest room.

'Yes, I'm sure it will,' said Dad, thinking of the decision that he and Sarah had made.

When her mother came back into the room Emma was saying, 'When I was little I was afraid of those bees but I used to watch them bravely from the guest room window.'

'What made you think of that, love?' Mother asked.

'I was thinking of Great-Grandma being in there.'

Mother came over to where Emma was sitting and put a gentle hand on her shoulder. 'Emma,' she said seriously, 'being part of a family is a good feeling, isn't it? We share our happy times like today, as well as our sad times. And we all know that if any of us is in trouble we can always rely on the family, don't we?'

'Yes, I know that,' Emma said.

'Sometimes we have to give up things we like doing for the sake of others and it isn't always easy.'

'Do you mean like you giving up your job when you married Dad?'

'Something like that,' Mother smiled, 'but there was

a lot of happiness too, wasn't there, Alan?'

'I should jolly well think so, Sarah,' he said smiling back at her.

Emma looked from one to the other and sighed. It was obvious that something was waiting to be said and she just wished they'd get on and say it.

'What Mother means is that we're going to build an extension at the back to make a self-contained flat for Great-Grandma,' he said.

'And that is going to mean you and Paul giving up the games room,' Mother finished.

The shock took Emma's breath away: she went white and her lips set into a thin tight line but she managed to control the tears which she could feel welling up. She just stood there looking at her parents. It was so unfair that it had to be *her* playroom that was being taken away; it was the only place where she and her friends could really be themselves. Girls at school still talked about going to 'Emma's room'. She'd been able to say '. . . we can get together in my room' the time when the carnival dragon had been sewn together with all its tassles and sequins; or the time when the whole floor had been littered with paper flowers and the maypole dancers had come to practise. All those times had made Emma feel proud that she had a 'place of her own', and now it wouldn't be the same any more.

'Now Emma, what's the matter?' said Dad gently.

Emma glared at him. Then with her lip trembling she said, 'It's not fair, I'm fed up and I'm going to bed.'

Mother put her arms out toward her but Emma was in no mood for a goodnight kiss and headed toward the door.

'You're tired, it's been a long day. Maybe you'll feel better about things when you've had time to sleep on it,' Mother said.

Emma left the room without answering, ran upstairs and flung herself on her bed. After about ten minutes of sulking and feeling sorry for herself her sensible side decided that she'd better get undressed before she fell asleep on top of the bed.

Then she snuggled down under the bedclothes but now she was wide awake again. She wanted to say her prayers but her head was full of jumbled thoughts and angry feelings so she thought it might be wiser to clean up those thoughts before she talked to Jesus.

She asked herself 'Who am I cross with?' and then tried to answer honestly. Emma found that she certainly wasn't cross with Great-Grandma because the old lady didn't know anything about the playroom. She wasn't even cross with Mum and Dad either because she knew that they were only trying their best to help Great-Grandma. So who did that leave? Just herself. Could she be cross with herself?

Suddenly she had the answer: there must be two selves; her best self and her worst self, both of them struggling to be 'Emma'. It was a strange idea but it made sense and she realised that downstairs when she'd glared at her parents and felt so furious it had been her worst self, the selfish part taking over. What a relief to have found out because now she could do something about it. Then she smiled as she realised that it was probably Jesus who had helped her to untie the knots in her mind.

Emma's prayers were hardly ever words spoken out loud because words take so long and don't ever say all you mean anyway; so when she prayed she would find a thought in her mind, like a tree thought, and let it collect together all the many surrounding thoughts, like branches, and send them to Jesus all in one mind-parcel.

Tonight's mind-parcel was about getting rid of

selfishness, and right at the very end of her prayers she added an after-thought in the words of the little song Jiminy Cricket had sung in the film Pinocchio.

'. . . when you don't know right from wrong, give a little whistle, and always let your conscience be your guide . . .'

Emma settled down to sleep with a warm glowing feeling of everything being all right again. She half wondered if she should go downstairs and tell Mum and Dad . . . but no, she could tell them in the morning.

3

Next morning Emma bounded downstairs two at a time and flung her arms around her mother's waist as she stood cooking breakfast.

'Watch out, bacon fat,' cautioned her mother and then added, 'You're bright eyed and bushy tailed this morning.'

Emma beamed at her, 'Very first of all, I'm sorry . . . about last night.'

'Well I must admit, you weren't your usual sweet self, were you?'

'That's just it, Mum, I worked it out last night in bed. It's as if there were two people inside me, my best self and my worst self; sometimes one wins and sometimes the other.'

Sarah raised her eyebrows as she served out the bacon and eggs then going to the back door she called down the garden to tell Alan that breakfast was ready.

'Tell me more, Emma, it sounds interesting,' said Sarah. 'Fanciful maybe but still interesting.'

Alan washed his hands under the tap and followed Sarah and Emma into the dining room.

'So you see,' Emma continued, turning to include Dad, '. . . last night the wrong self won the struggle and all I could think of was *my* playroom and what *I* wanted.'

Dad put on a mischievous face and said, 'She's not

28

going to visit us very often, is she?'

'Who?' said Sarah looking up.

'Why, this Greta Grotbox girl that wears our Emma's clothes now and then. I'm not very keen on her at all,' Dad said shaking his head sadly.

Emma gave a great hoot of laughter and spluttered into her orange juice.

'I'll try to keep her away,' Emma said after she'd calmed down. 'But if ever I'm horrid all you need to say is go-away-Greta-Grot.'

'I'll remember that. It's a deal,' said Dad.

After breakfast Alan asked if either of them were going to morning service. Sarah usually stayed to prepare lunch and then went in the evening but today she said, 'Let's all go this morning; we can have cold chicken salad for lunch.'

Emma and her mother sat together and Dad was sitting with all the other members of the choir. The service began: first the hymns and readings and then Rev Timms began the sermon. Emma sat quietly listening for most of the time but then a fly settled on the hat of the lady in front. Emma's attention wandered away from what she was hearing and onto what she was seeing. Her thoughts strayed and she began looking at ... of the other members of the congregation. T.... to be listening intently but Emma jus... of them ever had an unwanted Gr... their heads. Probably they had ... that it was none of her busine... she could do anything ab...

When they got home ... parents got out the ... passage towards th... them.

'As far as '

the side wall of the games room so there won't be any problem with the plumbing,' said Alan.

Mother opened the door and walked across the polished floor, her high heeled shoes sounding like a pony's hooves on the hard surface.

'We could build out here to make an entrance hall. That way she'd have her own front door.'

While Alan was taking some measurements he moved aside a large rubber plant; a ping-pong ball rolled out from behind the plant pot.

'Catch,' he said, throwing it in Emma's direction. She caught it with one hand and then saw the little crack on its dusty surface.

'So that was where it went,' she said softly to herself.

Emma stood in the middle of the floor and took what she knew to be a last look at what had been her playroom. She felt a twinge of sadness but that soon drifted away because she wouldn't allow it to stay.

'After today we mustn't call it the games room or the playroom because from now on it's Great-Grandma's flat,' she said, collecting up some of her things which she'd left lying about. 'Do you want me to write and tell Paul all about it?'

'Good girl, that's the spirit,' said Dad.

'I can tell that you're going to be a great help to me when it comes to choosing things for the new flat,' said Mother.

Emma smiled and nodded, then opening the garden
or she went outside. A few minutes later she was back
again.

see where the garage sticks out, well if you
cross to here it would mean that Great
an enclosed patio.'

he said, peering out of the

'Oh yes, I like that idea,' Sarah joined in. 'We could even put some beams across for hanging baskets, and on the patio we could have some tubs in shrubs.'

'Great Grandma would probably like them better the other way round,' Alan said, winking at Emma. 'Shrubs in tubs would be preferable.'

'Pardon? What did *I* say? Oh, go on with you, you knew what I meant,' Sarah said, shaking her fist at him.

Emma began to feel quite excited as the weeks passed. First there had been the plans drawn in black ink with a pale wash of water colour added; then, as soon as planning permission had been received, the builder's men arrived and began to turn those plans into reality. A cheerful little cement mixer, bright orange and very noisy, was set up near the back gate and the sound of its churning soon became a part of the day's routine.

Nearly every time Emma returned from school she noticed that something different had happened: what had once been a pile of bricks had turned into the entrance hall, and what had been a stack of timber had become the dividing walls making the various rooms in the flat.

One of Emma's jobs was to go round after the men finished for the day and collect up all the empty tea mugs she could find. They were left in the most peculiar places; she even saw one mug perched high up on the half-finished roof but she left it there rather than go scrambling along the scaffolding.

Mother had written long letters to Great-Grandma telling her in detail what was happening and asking her to choose from some colour schemes, but the next letter from Malaysia said: 'My dears, I leave it entirely up to you. I'm sure you have very good taste.'

Once the roof was on the entrance hall the work seemed to speed up inside the flat and, because space was so limited, many of the fitments had been cleverly designed to fold back into the wall. For the bathroom Dad had suggested a combined bath and shower unit and Emma and her mother chose shower curtains and wall tiles that toned with the avocado-coloured bathroom suite.

'It's a bit like living in a dolls' house,' Emma said one day as she discovered where the ironing board folded out from the wall. 'Everything is small and neat and folds away when it's finished with.'

One morning Emma came into the dining room where her mother had the sewing machine out; the colourful curtain material was draped in great swathes across the table.

'There's been nobody working in the flat since last week; is anything happening?' Emma said, looking worried.

'Since the painters and decorators left I've been in every day to open all the windows. We don't want the smell of paint clinging to these new curtains.'

'What about the carpets we chose?' Emma asked next.

'Someone is coming tomorrow to fit them and then we'll have the new furniture delivered,' replied Sarah calmly.

'There's only another week before Great-Grandma arrives. Will everything be ready in time?' Emma said anxiously.

'Don't worry, we'll make sure that everything is ready,' Sarah said as she sewed up the hem of the last curtain.

On the evening before the big day Emma picked some flowers from the garden and arranged them in two vases, one for Great-Grandma's living room and one for her bedroom. Her mother was in the kitchen making sure that basic stores were in the cupboard when Emma came in to fill the vases with water.

'Mum, can't I come to the airport with you? Please.'

'No, we've been through all this before,' her mother said patiently. 'The flight doesn't arrive until three o'clock and by the time we've driven back you'll be home from school anyway.'

'Oh, all right,' grumbled Emma, '. . . but it wouldn't hurt to have the afternoon off school. I could say I didn't feel well.'

'You will not,' her mother said sternly. 'And what's more, Miss Greta Grotbox, if you tell lies like that you might just wake up one day and find that you really were poorly and no one would believe you.'

Next day after breakfast Emma collected her school bag off the hall chair and then rushed into the kitchen. 'Don't forget to give me the key.'

The back door key with its little piece of string was handed over and Sarah gave her a big kiss. 'I'm so glad you're feeling well this morning,' she said with a grin.

'Yes, I'm going to school,' Emma said wearily, 'and I'll be waiting for you all from half past four onwards, is that right?'

'That's it, unless the flight is delayed.'

The day crawled past, seeming twice as long as usual, but at last the bell went. Emma hurried past everybody else and made a dash for the bicycle sheds with Lauren and Anita close behind her.

'You're in a galloping hurry,' Lauren said as they nearly collided.

'Are you coming to Leslie's for a while?' Anita asked.

'No, didn't I tell you? Great-Grandma arrives today,' Emma said, heaving her bicycle out of the rack.

'Goodness, is the playroom ready? . . . Sorry, I mean the flat,' Anita said.

'Yes, and it's really nice now it's finished,' Emma told them.

Lauren removed the lollipop from her mouth and waved it at Emma.

'It doesn't seem two minutes since you were showing us round the empty shell with all those builder's men banging and thumping about.'

'I must go. I don't want them to arrive home before I do.' Emma began to move away between the forest of bicycles.

'Tell us about it tomorrow,' the girls called after her.

'I will,' she promised.

Emma turned the key in the lock and opened the back door. It was too quiet in the kitchen; the emptiness was in such contrast to the usual welcoming warmth. She looked at the clock. It was just four o'clock, and in that same moment the oven timer clicked on and the cat-flap rattled.

Puddy called his usual greeting of prr-up and coiled himself sinuously around Emma's legs. She bent to pick him up and buried her nose in his soft fur.

'I hope Great-Grandma likes cats,' she said thoughtfully and it suddenly made her realise how little she knew about someone who would soon be sharing their lives.

Emma changed out of her school clothes, put on an apple green track suit and brushed her auburn hair back, securing it with a large green comb-clip. She looked at herself in the mirror and pulled a face at the crop of freckles that she saw reflected.

She went into the dining room and got out cups, saucers and little plates. Then, opening the display cabinet, she carefully removed the silver tea pot, milk jug and sugar basin. The silver things were mostly used on special occasions and Emma felt sure that today was such an occasion. Mother always left a few dry tea leaves inside this pot to 'keep it sweet' as she said. Filling the milk jug and sugar basin only took a few minutes and when she looked at the time it was still only twenty past four. She wandered around aimlessly for a while longer and then, just as she'd decided to get a book to read, she heard the car turn into the drive and the horn sounded.

Emma rushed to open the front door and ran towards the car. Then she stopped, her mouth open in surprise. Surely this couldn't be Great-Grandma? A tall thin figure was easing herself out from the back seat of the car; she had close cropped brown hair and she was wearing a tomato-red safari jacket and trousers. Anything more unlike a frail old lady it would have been hard to imagine.

Great-Grandma looked over to where Emma was standing and her sun-bronzed face broke into a wide smile.

'Emma, my dear,' she called in a deep loud voice, 'how wonderful to see you at last.'

Emma found herself almost lifted off the ground in the enthusiasm of Great-Grandma's bear-hug greeting. Remembering her manners she knew she had to say something, if only to give herself time to recover from the shock.

'Did you have a good journey?' she asked politely.

'Yes, fine. Well, to be truthful, no, it was ghastly but I'd rather not think about it until I've had a good rest,' Great-Grandma said, walking into the house.

'How about a cup of tea first, then we'll bring your cases in,' Alan suggested, opening the living room door for her.

'Wonderful. I think I shall sleep for a week once I sit down,' she laughed loudly as she lowered herself into an easy chair.

Emma ran ahead into the kitchen and when Sarah saw the tray all set out with the tea things ready she said, 'That was thoughtful of you, and you remembered the

35

silver spoons as well. Thanks, love.' The silver spoons had been part of the wedding present which Great-Grandma had given them.

'Mum, she isn't a bit how I thought she'd be!'

'Why, how had you pictured her?'

'Sort of frail and gentle like old people often are, but she doesn't really look old, does she?'

Sarah smiled, 'No she doesn't, in fact I'm surprised at how well she does look.'

As tea was being drunk Emma sat quietly listening and watching while the adults talked. She fetched more cakes and biscuits when she was asked and she removed Puddy when he nearly knocked a cup and saucer off the arm of a chair.

'You are very quiet,' Great-Grandma said at one point. 'Tell me all about yourself.'

Emma struggled to find words in answer to this sudden command. Great-Grandma's eyes were very bright and penetrating and they seemed to be looking right into Emma's head.

'Cat got your tongue?' she said jokingly.

'No, and he's called Puddy,' Emma said, feeling flustered but trying to make it into a joke too. 'Do you like cats?'

'Yes, they're nice little beasts. I prefer horses though; strong and noble animals. I had a horse called Wilson, I used to ride him all around the plantation. Do you ride?'

'Only a bicycle,' Emma replied.

That really seemed to amuse her and she laughed loudly. Then looking up she saw Alan standing in the doorway with a suitcase in each hand.

'Are you ready to see your new home?' he asked.

'Lead the way,' she replied, prising herself up from the depths of the easy chair.

The passage that used to lead to the back of the house had been turned into a long store cupboard and the connecting door had been blocked off. Now the only way into the flat was via its new front door. Sarah solemnly handed the flat's front door key to Great-Grandma and she opened her own front door for the first time and went inside.

She stood quite still for several moments looking at the bright and shining little home, and when she turned round Emma could see that there were tears in her eyes.

'Sarah and Alan, you are two very special people,' she said warmly. 'Thank you so much for everything. I'm delighted with my new home.'

Sarah put an arm across her daughter's shoulder. 'Emma helped to choose the furnishings, didn't you love?'

'Well thank you too, dear, and I wonder how you knew that pink is one of my favourite colours,' said Great-Grandma picking up one of the scatter cushions and running a finger around the frill.

'We'll leave you to unpack now and that'll give you a chance to poke about and find where everything is,' said Sarah, moving through into the kitchen. 'One or two things like sugar and tea, cereals and jam are in this cupboard and we can do a big shop-in tomorrow.'

Emma opened the fridge door. 'And milk and orange juice in here,' she said.

'One more thing,' Sarah said, taking Great-Grandma's arm and leading her back towards the entrance hall, 'Alan had this two-way internal call system fitted so . . . I'll give you a buzz when we're about to serve the meal. In about an hour if that's OK?'

Mother, Dad and Emma walked back along the covered way to their own back door. Dad had taken up Emma's suggestion about the low wall to enclose the patio but he had also had the builders construct a covered walkway open to the air on one side. Hanging baskets of pink geraniums and blue lobelia were just coming into flower and they looked beautiful against the white painted roof supports.

When the evening meal was ready Great-Grandma arrived at the kitchen door wearing a shimmering silk house-robe in shades of pink and purple. It was tied with a gilt sash and she wore slippers to match. She peeped round the door saying, 'Here I am, I heard the buzzer.'

Sarah nearly dropped the serving spoon in amazement.

'Sorry about the house-robe,' said Great-Grandma; '. . . but I didn't bring many clothes back with me. I had visions of snow and cold winds in England so I knew I'd need a complete new wardrobe anyway.'

'You will for the winter,' Sarah said, recovering from her surprise, '. . . but this is summer; nothing like the heat in Malaysia I know. Anyway you look very impressive in that.'

Emma was coming into the kitchen and had heard most of the conversation. She looked across at her remarkable relative from Malaysia and smiled to herself.

'It's real Chinese silk,' Great-Grandma continued, '. . . and I just had to bring this back with me, even if it is somewhat flamboyant.'

Emma gazed at her. The tomato-red safari suit had been unusual but this outfit looked like a page from a fashion magazine.

'Great-Grandma, you are full of surprises,' she said.

'Aren't I just,' said the old lady, laughing.

4

At school next day Emma told Lauren and Anita most of what had happened the evening before. She told them about how tall Great-Grandma was and about her loud voice. She described the unusual clothes she had worn and the way her hair was almost as short as a boy's, then she ended by saying, 'I don't mean that she looks young. It's just that she doesn't look old like I'd expected.'

'I'm looking forward to meeting her. From what you've said she sounds like Superwoman,' Lauren said laughing.

'But do you like her? How do you get on with her?' asked Anita.

'Of course I like her, she's just . . . different, that's all,' Emma said rather quickly.

However, the one thing that Emma kept as her own secret was that in fact Great-Grandma made her feel a bit uncomfortable. Those grey eyes that would suddenly fix on you could be rather frightening, and so was the deep voice that sounded out of place in a small house. Great-Grandma was overpowering . . . yes, that was the word, overpowering.

During the rest of the week Emma was always polite to Great-Grandma but tried to keep out of her way as much as possible. When Sunday morning arrived Dad asked Emma to go round and see if Great-Grandma wanted to come to morning service with them.

'Can't we buzz and ask her when she picks up the phone?' Emma said, hoping to avoid the mission.

'We could but I think it would be more polite to go round,' said Dad.

Emma looked at her watch. It was only eight o'clock. She set off across the patio so that first she could check if the bedroom curtains were drawn back. They were and Great-Grandma had opened the door even before Emma's finger touched the bell.

'Thought you'd catch me still snoozing, did you?' she laughed. 'Deary me no, I've been up since six o'clock.'

Emma looked at her in astonishment, wondering why anyone would get up so early at the weekend. Although Emma hadn't spoken Great-Grandma had seen the expression on her face.

'You're wondering why. So come inside and I'll tell you.'

Emma wiped her feet carefully on the doormat before she went in.

'I've never been a lie-a-bed. When your Great-Grandfather and I ran the plantation we were always up at the crack of dawn; the men started work early before the heat of the day grew too intense. Rising early has become a habit now.' Then changing the subject she said, 'Have you had breakfast yet?'

'Yes, thank you, Great-Grandma. Really I came to ask if you'd like to come to church with us this morning or go in the evening instead.' Emma delivered the message all in one breath and then looked up expectantly for an answer.

'And when do *you* go?'

'The evening, usually, but Dad goes both times because he's in the choir.'

Great-Grandma looked thoughtful and then having

made her decision she said, 'I'll come this morning. The problem is hats; do you wear them?'

'Some people do, but Mum doesn't,' Emma said, edging toward the door.

'What a relief, because I don't have one.' She laughed loudly then added, 'Buzz me when you're ready.'

Emma nodded and walked back along the covered way. She suddenly had a mental picture of Great-Grandma striding into church wearing that tomato-red safari suit, or even worse, the pink and purple house-robe. Emma shuddered at the very thought and sincerely hoped that Great-Grandma had bought something more suitable when she'd been shopping with Mother.

Emma need not have worried. When Great-Grandma climbed into the car she had on a plain white linen suit, and with an emerald green scarf loosely knotted around her neck and heavy gold ear-rings she really looked striking. Emma's powder-blue skirt and blouson top looked quite pale in comparison.

All went well until they began to sing the first hymn. From a little to Emma's left came the booming tones of Great-Grandma's contralto voice. She knew all the words of all the verses without looking at the hymn book and she could be heard above everyone else.

Emma felt her neck going red with horror. Everyone would know that 'the voice' had come with the York family, and one or two people nearby had already cast a quick glance in their direction. Mother didn't look at all worried, at least not on the surface, but to Emma the whole situation was frightful. She had never felt so embarrassed in all her life. Previously Emma had never counted how many hymns there were during a service but this time she was made very much aware of each one as Great-Grandma's voice rang out loud and clear.

After the service Robert Timms was standing at the

door smiling and talking to members of the congregation as they went out. Sarah introduced Great-Grandma as 'Mrs Gimbourne' and while Robert welcomed her to the parish Emma gave a quick smile and hurried out of the way. She ran down the path and caught up with Lauren and Anita but almost at the same moment some of the crowd from the Youth Club joined them.

'I see your frail little granny has arrived,' the boy from the Post Office said sarcastically.

'She's my *Great*-Grandma,' Emma said, giving him an icy stare.

'You can say that again, and she's got a great voice to go with it,' his sister said with a cheeky grin.

'Don't be so rude. Going to church doesn't seem to have done you two much good this morning,' Emma said sharply.

'We weren't being rude but you must admit she's not quite the quiet little old lady you told us was coming, is she?' said Andrew.

'She can't help being tall,' said Emma defensively '. . . and in any case she's far more interesting to talk to than you are.' And having delivered that thrust with her verbal sword she linked arms with Lauren and Anita and marched off round the side of the church.

'Don't let them upset you,' Lauren comforted '. . . but it was funny,' she added and a smile began to twitch at the corner of her mouth.

'What was?'

'That booming voice echoing out and the horrified look on your face,' Anita said, beginning to laugh.

'It wasn't funny for me. I felt so embarrassed I could have crawled under a pew,' Emma grunted. 'Oh do stop giggling and let's hurry. I don't want to bump into those two clowns again.'

Together they walked around the church and through

the lychgate that led down onto the village green.

'I think your Great-Grandma looked very smart anyway – even if her hair is a bit short,' Lauren said.

'Are you going to introduce us then?' asked Anita.

The three girls walked across the grass and towards the car park, but before they got there they saw the white suited figure of Great-Grandma purposefully heading toward the duck pond on the other side of the green. By the time they caught up with her she was leaning on the fence gazing fixedly at a group of ducks sailing serenely across the water. Emma waited until she turned round and then introduced Lauren and Anita.

'Hello, so you are Emma's friends. Pleased to meet you,' she said smiling down at them, and then she waved an arm in the direction of the ducks.

'Look at that, ducks on a pond, so typically English. It's a long time since I've seen a village green with ducks.'

None of the girls knew quite what to say so they remained silent.

'Has Emma told you I've been living in Malaysia? I left a village very much like this when I was twenty years old – a long time ago. England has changed a lot since then,' she said sadly.

Lauren and Anita were both thinking that Emma's description of her had been right: she was indeed different. They wanted to say something but when the old lady looked at them with those piercing eyes neither of them could think of anything sensible to say. Lauren was the first to recover.

'We knew about you from Emma's letter with the sealing wax. I hope you like living here.'

'Yes, I'm sure I shall grow to like it here.' Then Great-Grandma's eyes softened and twinkled as if she were remembering some joke. She turned to Emma and said,

'I thought the sealing wax might intrigue you; and it does seem to have made a lasting impression.' She paused a moment, raising her eyebrows, and waited to see if the word-play had been noticed.

Lauren nudged Emma's arm, 'Sealing wax. Impression . . . get it?'

'Oh, of course,' then she laughed. 'Great-Grandma, what did you make the heron mark with? Was it a ring?'

'No, it's a little stamp that my father used to carry on his watch chain. I'll show it to you when we get back.'

Anita was looking in the direction of the car park and saw that her parents were waving at her impatiently. 'I think I ought to go now. I'm glad to have met you,' she said to Great-Grandma and then she raced away across the grass.

'Off you both go as well,' Great-Grandma said to Lauren and Emma, 'I'll be along in a minute.'

That afternoon Emma went up to her room and sat in the window seat looking down onto the garden. This was the place she always came to when she needed to think. Today her thoughts were in such a muddle and she needed to ask Jesus to help her sort them out. After a quiet little prayer she slowly began to understand a little more clearly.

The first problem had been that she'd invented a person and had then been disappointed when Great-Grandma wasn't how she'd imagined her. Then there was the feeling of being overpowered by her and finally being so embarrassed by her in church that morning. Yet in spite of all those things Emma had a deep-down feeling that she was very fond of Great-Grandma. How was she going to get round all these problems?

Suddenly a whole collection of thoughts began to unfold. It must be very unsettling to leave your home and travel back to the country where you were born only to find that it had changed beyond recognition . . . only ducks on a pond remaining the same. Also, all the friends Great-Grandma must have made had had to be left behind in Malaysia whereas here she knew nobody except the family. Emma began to feel more and more sorry for Great-Grandma and also to feel rather ashamed of herself for not being kinder.

'So what does it matter if her hair is too short and she sings too loudly,' Emma said aloud to herself. 'That's the way she is; just like I'm the way I am.'

Having reached this conclusion she made a resolve to be a much kinder companion to Great-Grandma.

It wasn't until many weeks later that Emma discovered the reasons for many of the puzzling things about Great-Grandma. For instance: it isn't sensible to have long heavy hair in the heat of Malaysia, so she had kept her hair short to stay cool. And about her singing voice; apparently she and Great-Grandad had had a building erected on their land to be used as a church for the small Christian community; and since some of the Malay workers found the hymns difficult to understand Great-Grandma had used her strong contralto voice to encourage the tiny congregation to, as she put it, 'make a joyful noise to the Lord.'

As the days went by Emma came to know Great-Grandma better and grew to love her more. The old lady had a very odd sense of humour and Emma soon discovered that some things she said which had seemed sharp, or even fierce, were really Great-Grandma's way of poking gentle fun.

One day Great-Grandma said with a very stern face, 'It's not good enough Emma, it will have to stop. Don't talk to me as if I were one of those stiff old clocks that stand ticking in people's halls.'

For a split second Emma wondered whatever she'd

done wrong, but then she realised it was only said in fun so she relaxed.

'What do you mean Great-Grandma?'

'There you go again . . . GREAT-GRANDMA . . . it makes me sound enormously ancient and huge.'

'Then what shall I call you?' Emma asked.

Great-Grandma rubbed the side of her nose and closed her eyes while she considered the matter. 'I've got it, call me "Gamboo". Can you remember that?'

Emma repeated the strange name several times thinking that it was probably a foreign word. Then she said, 'Yes I can remember it but what does Gamboo mean?'

'Do you remember that photograph I sent of the gardener, the one with the rake? When he first came to work for us as a boy his English was not very good, he found it difficult getting his mouth round English words. He tried very hard to say our names but "Mr and Mrs Gimbourne" came out as "Messy Gamboo" . . . so I accepted that as my name.'

Emma began to laugh helplessly.

'Yes, for years I've been known as Messy Gamboo but . . .' she raised her hand and looked fierce '. . . you can omit the messy bit, do you understand?'

With a gurgle of merriment Emma gasped, 'Yes, Gamboo.'

'Not even if on occasions I am messy.'

'No, Gamboo,' Emma spluttered.

'Well, that's settled then,' she said, rubbing her hands together.

From then on all the family called her Gamboo and all their friends were told why.

It was a Saturday morning when the haulage van drew up at the front of the house. The driver rang the bell and Sarah went to the door.

'Mrs Gimbourne?' he enquired.

'No, but she lives at the flat. Is there a parcel for her?'

The van driver grinned, 'I should say so – more like four crates.'

Sarah opened her eyes wide and Emma wondered whatever Gamboo had been ordering from the shops that would fill four crates.

'I'll give her a buzz,' Emma said.

Gamboo came round immediately, looking very pleased, and after she'd had a word with the van driver he agreed that it might be better to take the van to the back gate, nearer to Gamboo's front door.

Mother and Emma waited on the patio with Gamboo and eventually the driver pushed the first crate up the path on a trolley. Three more crates soon followed.

'They look heavy,' said Sarah.

'What's inside? What have you bought?' Emma asked.

'Nothing, be patient, all in good time,' Gamboo said, disappearing into the kitchen in search of a hammer. Using the claw end to prise out the nails she lifted off the wooden lid and began removing the thick mat of padding which had protected the contents.

'Just a few of my treasures,' Gamboo said with obvious pleasure as she saw again the carefully wrapped items which had travelled half way round the world in the hold of a ship.

'I hope nothing got broken,' Sarah said.

'I shouldn't think so; Wan Li and I packed them very carefully.'

The first to be unwrapped was a cardboard tube and inside, neatly rolled, was a painting of an Egyptian Pharaoh. Emma touched it very gently with one finger.

'Is it very old?' she asked.

Gamboo smiled. 'No, it's a copy that my dear husband bought for me in Cairo. It's a likeness of Akhenaten and is painted on papyrus.'

'We did about that at school,' Emma said brightly. 'It's a reed that they used to flatten and use as paper; Miss Emery said that it was probably amongst the papyrus reeds that Moses was found, not bulrushes.'

Gamboo found the two lengths of wood which attached to the top and bottom of the papyrus picture so that it would hang flat against the wall.

'He was a very special man was Pharaoh Akhenaten; he tried to tell his people that there is only one God and although some people understood, the majority went back to worshipping animal-shaped gods.'

Emma looked surprised. 'I thought everybody knew that there is only one God. Even when different people call God by different names it is still the same one that they mean – isn't it?'

'You are a very wise young girl,' Gamboo said, smiling warmly at her. 'There are still a great many adults who haven't yet realised the truth of what you've just said.'

Emma looked again at the papyrus picture and then she said, 'I like the way they've drawn the sun with little hands coming out from it, as if it was giving sunshine to the people.'

'Yes, and it's a good way of saying . . .' but then Gamboo stopped. 'Well, perhaps you can think of why Akhenaten chose that symbol to represent one God?'

Emma was quiet for several moments before answering. 'Is it because there would be nothing alive on earth without the sun?'

'Precisely. Just as there would be nothing in existence anywhere without God, would there?'

One by one an assortment of strange, beautiful and mysterious objects were unpacked all over the hall floor. There were painted wooden masks and a skin-covered drum from Africa, there was a pair of blue Chinese temple dogs, each one with its front paw on a ball and a very fierce expression on its face: in fact there were so many interesting things that Emma didn't know which to look at first.

Suddenly Sarah said, 'I'll go and make soup and toast for us all, shall I? All this unpacking has made me hungry.'

'Thanks dear, lovely,' said Gamboo.

In the last packing case there were only three items: a rocking chair, a small framed picture and a large bronze elephant. Emma stroked the cold metal curve of his trunk and patted the smooth back.

'Where is he going?' she asked.

'Here,' said Gamboo, standing the elephant against the wall. 'He can be a door-stop and hold open the front door on sunny days.'

Picking up the small framed picture Emma stood, her attention fixed upon the scene it was showing. There by the doorway a figure was standing. He carried a lantern in one hand and he was knocking on the door.

'This is lovely. He has a kind face,' said Emma passing it into Gamboo's outstretched hand.

Gamboo walked into the bedroom and chose a place for the picture.

'This is my most treasured possession, I've had it ever since I was a girl. Yes I think I'll hang it where I can see it from my bed,' she said tapping a picture hanger into the wall. Then she hung the picture and stood back, looking to see if it was straight.

'A man named Holman Hunt painted it. He called it the Light of the World.'

'Is it meant to be Jesus?' Emma asked.

'You are right, that is exactly who it is, and this picture is also a kind of symbol. It has a meaning behind it too, like the sun with hands.'

'Tell me about it, please,' said Emma sitting down on

the bed end.

Gamboo sat next to her. 'There is someone living behind that door and they hear Jesus knocking. Now, that person has a choice, either to pretend he hasn't heard and take no notice or . . . to open the door and invite Jesus with his lantern into his home . . . or her home.'

Emma began to smile slowly as she saw quite well what it meant.

'But it doesn't really mean a door and a house does it? The house is you or me and the door is . . . a way in.'

'Yes, that is a good way of putting it, I like that thought, don't you?' said Gamboo.

Just then the buzzer sounded and Emma skipped down the hall.

'Come on, Gamboo, soup and toast,' she called.

5

'When am I going to meet this brother of yours?' Gamboo said one day.

'Quite soon. Paul's school always finishes for the summer holidays before mine. It isn't fair,' Emma grumbled.

Gamboo began to knead the dough on a floured board, pushing her knuckles into the stretching mixture with the skill of practice. Emma loved to come round when it was baking day, the kitchen always smelled so delightfully warm and spicy. Gamboo enjoyed making her own bread, spice buns and cakes because she'd always done so. As she said, there was no corner shop on a rubber plantation. Emma watched as the ball of dough was covered with a cloth and left in a warm place to 'prove', doubling in size as the yeast made it rise.

'Tell me about Paul. Is he like you?'

'No, did you see last year's holiday photos? He's more like Dad, fair hair and blue eyes. Or did you mean what he's like as a person?'

'That's what I meant,' said Gamboo.

'He's fifteen and a tease, always playing tricks on me, but he's not bad as brothers go I suppose. I think he wants to train to be a vet.'

Gamboo dusted the flour off her elbows and smiled. 'In that case he and I are sure to get on well together.

I've always been interested in animals. That reminds me, your Puddy kitten came to visit me this morning.'

'I thought I hadn't seen him about at home,' Emma replied.

'He found a warm spot where the sun shines onto my bedroom carpet and he's been lying there ever since.'

When the dough had risen Gamboo filled the bread tins and then made the teacakes and spice buns while Emma tidied the kitchen worktops and put things away for her.

'You had a cat, didn't you?' Emma said, knowing the answer but asking the question just to start Gamboo off telling one of her stories.

'I've had several but Tigger was the most memorable. She was a huge tabby cat but very quick on her feet in spite of her size.' Gamboo put the last of the baking trays in the oven and then she sat down for a rest.

'Yes, Tigger was a brave cat and a good mother too. She had her kittens in the outside storeroom and one day a snake got in and threatened to kill them, but Tigger fought and fought to protect those kittens until she was quite exhausted. It was being so nimble on her feet that saved her, she always managed to keep just out of reach of its fangs.'

'Was it a big snake?'

'No, but very poisonous if it had bitten her.'

'Then what happened?'

'Fortunately one of the men came in, saw what was happening, and banged on an empty bucket with a stick. Snakes don't like loud noises, the vibrations bother them, so it turned and slithered away through a crack in the wall.'

'And was Tigger all right afterwards?'

'Oh yes, she soon revived and all her kittens grew up to be fine healthy cats like their mother.'

Emma loved to hear these tales of things that had happened during Gamboo's life in Malaysia and elsewhere. She had a way of making the details so vivid that it was almost like being there.

'Tell me some more things please, Gamboo,' Emma pleaded, resting her elbows on the table and looking as though she intended staying there for a long time.

'First of all let me take the bread out of the oven. Then we'll see.'

Gamboo tipped each loaf out and tapped the bottom, listening to the sound it made. She told Emma that she could tell if a loaf was cooked properly by the thud her knuckles made on its crusty base. After putting all her baking on wire trays to cool Gamboo made two mugs of coffee and came back to sit at the table.

Emma's eyes were drawn towards the currant teacakes that rested so temptingly just beyond her reach.

'No Emma, they'd give you tummy ache. Wait until they're cool,' Gamboo said, moving the wire tray even further along the table.

Emma smiled, took a sip of her coffee, and peered at Gamboo over the rim of her mug.

'What was I telling you about?' said Gamboo.

'Snakes,' prompted Emma.

'Oh yes, let me think a minute. Did I tell you about the strange affair of the snake and the ants?'

Emma shook her head.

'Not the little tidgy ants that live in English gardens but huge fellows with black heads and enormous jaws. They call them soldier ants, probably because they go on long marches through the undergrowth. Anyway, I came out of the house and noticed a large snake lying on the path; it was obviously dead but whether from natural causes or foul play I didn't stop to investigate. I was late and hadn't time to remove it so I left it lying there. When I returned about an hour later the snake had vanished. Thinking that the gardener had got rid of it I thanked him, but he said . . . "Me no touch snake, him go, Messy Gamboo" . . . So, where do you think it was?' Gamboo said mysteriously.

Emma laughed at the way she'd made her voice sound squeaky and high.

'Perhaps the snake wasn't dead after all,' she suggested.

'That's what we thought at first but in case it was wounded we had a good look around the garden. One thing I forgot to mention is that there were deep storm drains running all through our property . . . they needed to be deep because when the monsoons came the rain water rushed down those drains in torrents. But this was the dry season and so the storm drain was empty except for . . . the snake . . . which seemed to be gliding along very slowly.'

'Was it only wounded then?'

'No, it was quite dead. It was only moving because thousands upon thousands of ants were dragging, carrying . . . whatever you want to call it they were certainly marching it along back to their nest.'

'Poor snake,' said Emma.

'Why poor snake? He was dead, it didn't hurt him any more,' Gamboo said.

'I mean I'm always sorry when things have to die.'

'But dying is part of living, it's natural. And it would be a very full world if nothing ever died, wouldn't it?' Gamboo said cheerfully.

Emma didn't reply for several minutes then she said, 'I suppose so.'

'By the way, did you know you had an ant's nest in this garden? I think I've found the main entrance too.'

'A nest here? How big is it?' Emma looked interested.

Gamboo smiled. 'We aren't able to see how big it is because it's underground but we can follow the worker ants and see where most of them return to after they've found food. They are very busy little people and all have their different jobs to do. Some look after the babies, some keep the nest clean and some go out foraging for food. To call it a nest is a bit misleading. It's more like a city with different levels, galleries and passages.'

'Will you show me where it is, please.' Emma jumped up and was opening the door even before Gamboo had time to reply.

'Wait a minute, take some of this first,' said Gamboo, holding out the sugar basin. Emma looked surprised but put a spoonful into the palm of her hand as Gamboo showed her.

'If we leave some little trails we can watch what happens,' Gamboo said as she went outside, '. . . but don't leave any sugar near my door, I don't want any of them visiting my kitchen.'

Three little trails led to a small mound of sugar scattered on the garden path. Gamboo and Emma crouched down on the grass and waited patiently to see what would happen next. It was about four minutes before the first ant came along the sugar trail and found the mound. It twiddled its antenna, tested the sugar, then scuttled away through the grass.

'There you are,' Gamboo laughed. 'Now that ant will head straight for home and tell all his relations that a new restaurant has opened, and it won't be long before the rest of the family arrive.'

Together they watched in silence and at last Emma saw the column of ants approaching, first a few, then a few more and then a steady stream all advancing upon the sugar mound. Emma bent down very close to the ground so that she could see more clearly.

'When you really look closely at one it's beautifully made,' Emma said.

'I agree with you,' Gamboo replied. 'Everything that God has made is beautiful if you know how to look at it.'

Emma began to follow the ants' return journey, each ant carrying a tiny white sugar grain, she supposed. 'They are disappearing down a hole in this concrete base that holds the clothes dryer,' Emma called out from the other end of the garden.

'How odd, that isn't where they went when I first saw them,' replied Gamboo, hurrying over.

Both Emma and Gamboo were down on their hands and knees in the grass when the back gate clicked open and in came Anita and Lauren. The look of surprise on their faces was understandable in the circumstances. Although they'd both come to know Gamboo quite well by this time she had always been a dignified person, and certainly not given to crawling around the garden on all fours.

'Good afternoon, ladies,' Gamboo remarked as she resumed her full height.

'We've been following ants on a sugar trail,' Emma explained.

The two girls peered into the grass in the place where Emma was pointing.

Anita shuddered. 'They're creepy . . . and they bite.'

'They only nip if you annoy them first,' Emma said, putting her thumb in the path of an advancing ant. It stopped, waved its antenna, then scuttled off in the opposite direction.

'There, you see,' Gamboo said. 'Most wild creatures would rather avoid man than confront him. Human beings have a bad reputation for not fighting fair.'

'What do you mean by not fighting fair? We don't

56

fight with animals, do we?' said Lauren.

Gamboo looked at her and raised her eyebrows questioningly.

'Imagine that you had two eyes and one horn and you were set upon from a distance by a creature with two eyes and a telescopic sight on his rifle. Is that fair fighting?'

'No, when you put it like that it isn't fair,' Lauren agreed.

'Gamboo, what has two eyes but only one horn?' Emma asked.

Anita pretended to paw the ground with her hoof and said, 'A unicorn.'

'No, seriously, I can't think of an animal with only one horn,' said Emma.

'When Great-Grandad and I were in India there were still quite a number of Asian rhinoceros living in the wild. Most rhinos have two horns but the Asian rhino has only one; and there was a lot of trouble with poachers killing the animals for the horn which could be sold for a lot of money. Now there are no Asian rhinos left in India or Nepal.'

'That is terrible,' Lauren said. 'Can't anybody stop the poachers?'

Gamboo sighed and looked at each of the girls in turn. 'It's difficult to stop greedy men but the game wardens are trying to prevent more poaching.'

'You know a lot about animals, don't you?' Lauren said quietly.

'I've had a lot of years in which to learn,' Gamboo replied. 'You see, Mr Gimbourne and I visited many countries and we always enjoyed discovering the wild animals and how they lived. It seems to me that God placed men and women and animals all on the same world together so we really ought to learn as much as we can about them. What do you think?'

'Yes, but not everybody can go and visit foreign countries though, even if they want to,' Anita said.

'That's true,' said Gamboo, 'but there are places in this country where people can meet wild animals.'

'A zoo,' said Anita.

'Or a safari park,' said Lauren.

'Yes, I was thinking of a safari park; there the animals are free to wander about and it's a little more like their natural life style,' Gamboo said.

The three girls looked at each other and then at Gamboo. Once the idea had been put into their minds it seemed more and more exciting.

'Could we?' Emma begged.

'Could we all go?' added Lauren.

'Together?' finished Anita.

Gamboo hadn't really meant to set this project in motion but she could see that all three of them were full of expectation.

'I'm not making any promises,' Gamboo said cautiously. 'I'm perfectly willing to take you but . . . it all depends on whether your parents would let you go.'

The idea had taken a firm hold of their imagination and within a few days Anita and Lauren had persuaded their parents that they would be quite safe even though animals were roaming free, and they explained that visitors never get out of their cars. It was agreed by everyone that Gamboo was just the right person to tell them about the animals, and after several phone calls all the plans were made and a date was fixed during the first week of the holidays.

Before this event however came an equally exciting day in the York family – Paul's return from boarding school. His train was to arrive at six o'clock on the Friday evening and it had become family tradition that on his return the whole family went out for a meal to celebrate.

When Gamboo was told she said it would probably be better if she didn't come with them this time.

'Why ever not, Gamboo,' Emma said, looking very surprised. 'I thought you'd enjoy a meal out. It's a family occasion and you are part of the family, so why don't you want to come?'

Gamboo gave a deep chuckle and then she said, 'I remember your little face when we first met. You didn't know quite what to make of me, did you?'

Emma blushed and looked down at the toes of her shoes.

'I didn't realise that it was so obvious,' she half whispered.

Gamboo patted her gently on the shoulder. 'Don't worry, I wasn't offended. And it didn't take you long to find out that your Great-Grandma wasn't such a funny old onion after all. So, let Paul have his home-coming meal with his family first and then he can face the shock of meeting me later.'

When the family met Paul off the train they were all a little surprised at how much he had changed since the beginning of term. He seemed taller and thinner and his fair hair was beginning to curl onto the collar of his leather jacket. In response to Alan's raised eyebrows Paul said, 'I know, I need a haircut.'

'I wasn't going to say that,' his father said, 'I was just thinking that you'll soon be as tall as I am.'

It turned out to be a very happy evening and Paul had them all laughing so much that they could hardly eat their food. He told funny stories about the cricket team and of acting mishaps in the drama club until Emma began to wonder when they found time to do any school work. On the way home Paul suddenly asked the question that Emma had been expecting all evening.

'Where's Great-Grandma and why didn't she come? You did ask her?'

Before Emma could think of the right way to explain Dad said, 'She thought the shock of meeting her might put you off your food,' and he managed to say it with a straight face.

'Nothing puts me off my food,' Paul grinned, 'but you haven't answered my question.'

Sarah scowled at her husband and scolded, 'Alan, don't say such awful things, it's not like that at all and well you know it.' Dad just grinned.

'What she said was that you should have the meal with us as usual and you could meet her later,' Emma explained, '. . . and call her Gamboo, not Great-Grandma. I told you about that.'

In her letters to Paul, Emma had told him all sorts of things about what Gamboo had said and done, so he almost felt as though he knew her already. And on Saturday morning when he was going round to the flat Emma called out, 'Shall I come too?'

'Not this morning,' he said cheerfully, 'This is my time.'

Emma knew exactly what he meant. Even so she was eager to hear from him as soon as he came back.

'What did you talk about?' she asked, bubbling with curiosity.

'Your name came up one or twice, Freckle Face,' said Paul.

'Stop teasing and tell me . . . unless it's a secret.'

'No secrets. We talked about India and the Far East mostly. Did you know that she and Great-Grandad once raised a baby elephant that had lost its mother?'

Emma shook her head. 'No, she hasn't told me that one, I must ask her.'

'Tell me, sis, had you talked about me wanting to go in

for veterinary work? It was just that every conversation seemed to end up talking about unfortunate animals . . . which I thought was rather odd.'

'I think I might have mentioned it,' Emma admitted.

'That explains it then,' Paul said, opening the biscuit tin and helping himself. Emma looked at him askance.

'What's the matter, is there a law against eating biscuits?'

'Well, it's nice to be asked,' Emma said.

'Sorry. Have half then,' he said, pushing a couple of biscuits into her hand. 'There was something else I was going to say.' He paused to think. 'Oh yes, Gamboo told me about the plan to visit Sarmesworth Safari Park; that sounds like fun.'

Emma poured out a glass of lemonade for herself and Paul, handed him his and then propped herself against the fridge with one foot on a stool.

'That's right, next week after we break up from school. It's going to be a great day,' she said.

There was a long pause and a prickling silence which Emma pretended to ignore, but she had to look across at him eventually. Paul pulled a most peculiar face at her.

'What are you looking like that for?' she said.

'Just waiting,' he said gazing up at the ceiling.

Emma began to giggle, she just couldn't help it. 'Waiting to be asked I suppose. OK. Do you want to come with us?'

'I thought you'd never ask,' he laughed. 'But seriously, I've been wanting to go to that place ever since it opened; and I dare say I can put up with you and your buddies just for once.' He quickly ducked behind the kitchen door.

'What a cheek. If we can put up with you is more like it,' Emma called after him.

He was soon back in the kitchen to return the empty

lemonade glass.

'She's a great character is Gamboo. Somehow she makes you feel more like a friend that a relation,' Paul said.

'I know, I love her too,' Emma replied.

There was only one more day before the trip to the safari park and that afternoon Gamboo buzzed on the internal phone asking Paul and Emma to come round. When she opened the door it was obvious that she was dressed for going out.

'I wondered if either of you wanted to come with me to collect the van?' she said and then she laughed. 'Whatever is the matter? You're both staring at me with eyes as big as barn owls.'

'What van, Gamboo?' said Emma looking bewildered.

'Why the one I've hired for tomorrow, of course.'

'I didn't realise that you were driving us there,' Paul said.

'My dear boy, I've driven a ten-ton truck half way across Borneo so I don't think a trip to Sarmesworth should overtax my strength.'

Paul grinned and said, 'We'll both come with you.'

They took the bus into town, collected the blue and white camper van and returned home in triumph. Gamboo had decided that if they were going to a safari park they might as well make the visit into a real mini-safari: she bought food to cook on the bottle gas stove, ice cream and cans of fruit juice to keep in the little fridge and three rolls of film to put in her camera.

Next morning at half past six Paul and Emma crept quietly out of the house and joined Gamboo at the camper van in the back lane.

She had already packed mugs, plates and other utensils and was now busy filling the water tank which fed water through a pump into the little sink. By seven o'clock

62

they had called for both Lauren and Anita and were bowling along the motorway at a good speed.

'It's a good thing you hired a camper van, there's loads of room back here,' Lauren shouted above the noise of the engine.

'We'd have been squashed in an ordinary car,' agreed Emma.

'When your Gamboo goes on safari she goes in style,' she called back from the driving seat.

By half past eight they had arrived at the front entrance of Sarmesworth Safari Park only to find that they were too early. The gates weren't open. However, it didn't matter; they parked on the grass verge, extended the roof section and made themselves toast and honey. Paul pumped away frantically and got nothing but air from the tap at first but eventually he got enough water flowing to make a pot of coffee. When an official knocked on the window to tell them that they really shouldn't be camping there Gamboo explained, offered him a mug of coffee and engaged him in a long conversation about keeping baboons. He opened the gates nearly half an hour early and let them inside.

Once they'd paid the entrance fee there was no time limit. They had a whole day of adventure ahead of them. They could go anywhere they liked as long as they kept to the roadway, and notices said that they must NOT get out of their vehicle for any reason at all.

As they made their way slowly into the wooded area they kept a sharp look-out for lions. Emma was the first to see one and whispered, 'Look over there, resting under that tree.'

Everybody laughed at her for whispering and Paul said, 'I don't think he'd hear even if you shouted, he's at least a hundred yards away.'

'He's quite an elderly gentleman,' said Gamboo, 'and

probably as deaf as a post.'

There was still dew on the grass and it shimmered in the early morning sunlight. They were so busy thinking how beautiful everything was, and watching the old lion rolling over in the grass like an overgrown kitten, that nobody noticed a lioness and her three cubs come wandering across the road towards the camper van. Suddenly Anita let out a strangled squeal.

'Are they going to attack us?' she managed to say.

The lioness passed by on the driver's side, gave Gamboo a sidelong glance and made a low growling purr from deep within her throat.

'She's just calling to her cubs,' Gamboo said. 'This lady wouldn't need to attack us for food, she's far too sleek and well fed.'

The cameras went click several times before the lion family passed out of clear view. There was plenty of opportunity for taking some really close-up photographs during the morning. They saw several groups of lions in their wooded area, and then down across the level plain was an odd assortment of hoofed animals in small groups; deer, goats, zebra, llamas and bison – all very different in appearance but sharing the common necessity of eating a lot of grass each day.

Lauren made a startling observation which later had everyone smiling: she said she'd seen an enormous zebra which was almost as big as an elephant.

'There it is again, look. I knew I was right,' she said forcefully. But then everybody else saw it too and the laughter rang out. There coming through between the trees was a vehicle painted white with black zebra markings. It was the park ranger's van and he'd been doing his routine inspection of the stock fencing, making sure that all the enclosures were safely divided off from one another.

As it happened it was the man they'd seen that morning at the gates and he waved cheerfully at Gamboo as his zebra van lurched back up onto the roadway.

Another highlight of the day was the cowboy dinners that Gamboo cooked for them on the little stove. In the safety of the car park they got out to stretch their legs and play frisbee and then they sat on the grass to eat a delicious meal of sausage, bacon, beans and tomato.

And then there were the monkeys. Gamboo yelled, 'Watch out!' as she slammed on the brakes, and apples and coffee mugs cascaded onto the back seat.

'What's happening?' Emma cried out, nursing her bumped nose.

'The silly things ran across the road in front of us,' Paul said. 'I don't know how you managed to miss them, Gamboo.'

Other families were also having problems with the monkeys who by now were leaping up onto the roofs and windscreens of cars. One poor man was watching in horror from inside his car while a chattering monkey pulled and tugged at the windscreen wipers.

'It'll break them off if it goes on like that,' Emma said.

'Pass me an apple,' said Gamboo, then she opened the window and threw the apple onto the road. Her plan worked. The monkey jumped down to retrieve the fruit and the car owner drove away, giving Gamboo a grateful pip on the horn as he went.

At last their long and happy day at Sarmesworth came to an end. They drove back along the motorway and arrived in the village just as the crimson sun sank below the horizon.

6

Nearly all Gamboo's photographs came out very well and Emma was also quite pleased with the ones she had taken. She had tried to get some shots of animals while they were moving but these were rather disappointing, being fuzzy and blurred at the edges. When Paul saw the photos he made technical remarks about 'apertures' and 'shutter speed' which Emma didn't find particularly helpful, so she got out her bicycle and went over to Lauren's house with her photos.

Lauren hadn't taken a camera with her to the safari park so she had tried to do something different to keep a record of her day out.

'When I saw something I wanted to remember I pretended to click a camera somewhere behind my eyes,' she said, looking at Emma to see if she thought the idea silly, '. . . and then when I got home I tried to draw them.'

'Good idea, and did it work out?' Emma laughed.

'Half and half,' Lauren said, hunting through her cupboard for the pieces of paper. 'These are the better ones that I didn't tear up.'

Emma looked carefully at the pencil sketches of monkeys, lions and zebra and then she smiled. 'You've even got that haughty look on this camel's face. They're very good, but then you're always better than me in art lessons.'

Later Emma went back home determined to try the same thing herself; she thought it might be easier if she used the photos to jog her memory though. She spent hours up in her room, her table top spread with paper, pencils, rubbers and water colour paints . . . and her tongue poking out of the corner of her mouth in the effort of concentration. There was a pile of drawings and paintings by the end of the day. Some were reasonably life-like but she simply couldn't make the animals look as though they were moving. She felt quite disheartened about it.

Dad said, 'They're lovely, dear,' but then he always admitted that he couldn't even draw a straight line. Mother said, 'I like your use of colour,' and Paul said, 'That tiger has got no bones in its body.'

His remark was a bit unkind, but accurate. Emma looked again at her painting and secretly wondered what Paul's pictures had been like when he was only twelve years old.

'Mind you,' he added cheerfully, 'it's a better tiger than I could do – even now.'

Emma went up to bed feeling less disheartened.

First thing next morning she went round to see Gamboo, taking her paintings and drawings with her. Gamboo was quite an accomplished artist and had had several of her paintings of orchids exhibited in Singapore. Each waxy petal was recreated in lovingly observed detail and the blooms looked so real that you felt you could reach into the picture and lift a flower out. Emma often looked at them as they hung on Gamboo's living room wall and wished she could paint as well as that.

'Please will you look at these and tell me what's wrong. I can't make them look right,' Emma said, handing her drawings to Gamboo one by one. Gamboo didn't just flick through them, she spent a long time looking at each one and at last she said, 'I like the way you use brush strokes and you have a good eye for colour.'

'That's what Mum said too. However, Paul said my tiger was boneless.'

'Well, dear, he doesn't stand up for himself, does he? The tiger I mean, not Paul . . . but it's a very good attempt.'

Emma wandered around the room looking for a pencil because she'd forgotten to bring one with her; she found one near the telephone and brought it to Gamboo.

'Perhaps you could show me how to make them move. All my animals look stiff and awkward.'

Gamboo took one of the papers that had hardly any drawing on it and with one or two quick strokes she formed the outline of a tiger.

'This one is lying at rest, see how all the lines are soft, curved and sleepy.' Then taking the pencil again she sketched in a leaping tiger, the sharp angled lines of his legs and tail creating the impression of movement. 'And these lines are about hard bones and muscles,' Gamboo explained.

'Yes but how do you *do* it?' Emma groaned.

'In one way Paul was right. In order to draw an animal, or a person, in movement you do have to know where the bones are . . . what the skeleton is like.'

Emma thought for a moment and then said, 'Like matchstick men?'

'That's right, and there is an easy way to find out how bones move; shall I show you?'

Emma nodded enthusiastically.

'Very well. Go into the garden and collect some small twigs as thick as your little finger.'

'Aren't you coming outside with me?'

'Not just now, love, I'm feeling a bit tired. Also it'll

give me time to find that plasticine . . . I'm sure I had some left.'

Emma looked at Gamboo and smiled. 'I'll be back as soon as I've got the sticks,' she said and ran out through the open door.

The suitcase that Gamboo wanted was right at the back of the broom cupboard and while she was reaching for it she suddenly felt very dizzy. Putting out a hand to save herself from falling she bumped into one of the shelf units; buckets and scrubbing brushes crashed down onto the floor and the shoe cleaning kit scattered its contents all around. A tin of shoe polish began to roll and as Emma came into the kitchen the tin rolled right up to her feet.

'Are you all right, Gamboo?' she said, pulling the cupboard door wider open.

'I had a dizzy spell and lost my balance, that's all. I'll be fine again once I've sat down.'

Emma picked up the things that had fallen off the shelf and was just about to shut the cupboard when Gamboo got hold of Emma's arm to steady herself.

'Do you think you could reach down that old green suitcase for me?' she said.

While Gamboo went to sit down in the living room Emma pulled the case down and heaved it out from the back of the cupboard. It was heavy and something inside it rattled.

Gamboo still looked rather shaken and not her usual bright self but she managed a smile when Emma came in carrying the case.

'Put it down here and then you can open it for me,' said Gamboo.

Emma clicked open the two brass locks and pushed back the lid. Inside was a treasure chest of artist's materials: there were pastel crayons and blocks of paper, two small canvases on stretchers and a toffee tin full of tubes of oil paint – they were the things that had rattled.

'Aren't there some boxes of plasticine?' Gamboo asked.

Emma delved deeper into the case and pulled out a box of stone-coloured plasticine, the cardboard stained with oil which had seeped out.

'What did you need this for? I thought only children used plasticine for making things,' Emma laughed.

'I used to take a lump, make it into a sort of thumb pot then put a few drops of water at the bottom; it was ideal for holding my orchid specimens while I painted them.'

'That was a bright idea,' Emma said, '. . . but what is this down here?' She lifted out a square box with a tight-fitting lid and looked at Gamboo.

'Yes, you can open it,' Gamboo nodded.

Carefully prising off the lid Emma folded back the lining paper and saw a strange little wooden figure. The head was egg-shaped but without a face and the two-piece body had jointed arms and legs with flat hands and feet attached.

'Who is this little man?' said Emma, taking him out of his box.

Gamboo held out her hand and Emma gave him to her.

'This is Claude; he is what they call a lay-figure. Artists use them when they want to see the right position to draw a body.'

Gamboo reached into the box and produced the stand onto which she fastened Claude, then she altered the arms and legs, the waist and neck, making him run, bend over or jump . . . whatever position she wanted.

'That's really neat,' Emma said, appreciating the simple but effective help that Claude could give.

'And I imagine you've guessed by now what the sticks and plasticine are for,' Gamboo laughed.

'Right,' said Emma. 'Let's make an animal one.' Then she stopped and looked earnestly into Gamboo's face. 'Are you feeling better now? Or do you want me to make you a cup of tea or something first?'

Gamboo smiled and made Claude point toward the kitchen with his little wooden hand. 'I'm feeling as right as rain now, thank you, but I'd love a cup of tea.'

Emma went into the kitchen and it wasn't very long before she returned with a cup of tea for Gamboo and an ice-cream soda for herself. Gamboo had already softened the plasticine in her hands and was busy rolling several pieces into small balls each about the size of a gooseberry.

'I'll watch you first and then I'll make another one,' said Emma.

'Well, all animals are built along similar lines and their bone structure is fairly common sense when you think it out.'

Emma giggled. 'Bones hold it up and skin keeps it in.'

'Correct,' said Gamboo, breaking some of the twigs into more manageable sizes, then she began connecting them with plasticine joints. 'Start with a backbone or spine . . . a neck and a head.'

'Skull,' corrected Emma.

'Correct again, give it its proper name . . . skull. Now legs come in three pieces . . . thigh bone, leg bone and foot. So, we'll make these four legs and stick one at each corner.' Gamboo triumphantly stood the little stick skeleton firmly on its feet.

'What about a tail?' said Emma.

'Of course there are bones in its tail too but I don't think we need to bother making that, because you know how to draw a tail.'

Emma rolled some more plasticine into balls like Gamboo had done, broke some twigs into smaller sections and began to make her animal skeleton. When she'd finished she stood it proudly on the carpet beside the other one.

'How's that then? It's fitted together,' said Emma.

Gamboo bent forward in her chair to get a better view and then she laughed. 'It's easy to see which animal you were thinking about. A little skull on a long neck quite clearly says . . . giraffe.'

During the next few weeks Emma spent every spare minute practising drawing with the help of her little stick animals and she could see for herself that her drawings now had more life and movement. Gamboo suggested that she should try drawing people and she let Emma borrow Claude after she'd promised to take great care of him.

'He's almost as old as I am,' Gamboo told her one day, 'and he was given to me by a painter I knew when I was in Paris.'

'Is that why you call it Claude – after the painter?' Emma asked.

'Yes, and it was Claude Dubois who introduced me to your great-grandad all those years ago,' Gamboo said and a far-away look came into her eyes. 'I remember the little cafés with tables out on the pavements where we used to sit talking and drinking coffee while the whole world passed by – or so it seemed. Such happy times,' Gamboo sighed.

Emma waited patiently for a little while, expecting Gamboo to say something else and hoping that she was going to tell her about her time in Paris. But when Emma looked at her again Gamboo's eyes had closed and she had dropped off to sleep. Without disturbing her Emma tiptoed out of the room and went back home.

Mother met her at the kitchen door and said, 'Would you just pop back and asked Gamboo if she's finished her books. I'm going to the library. See if she wants to come with me.'

'She's asleep Mum, it was strange, one minute she was talking to me and the next minute she'd dozed off.'

'Oh, I'll sort out about the library books later then,' Sarah frowned and looked rather worried. Then she said, 'She would insist on cutting that back lawn even though I told her Dad would do it later. We must be more careful. I expect she's tired herself out; it's my fault for letting her do the lawn.'

'But that wouldn't tire her surely? It's an electric mower and all you have to do is keep it straight,' Emma said, remembering the time she hadn't held on firmly enough and it had chopped off the heads of some border plants. Dad had not been too pleased.

'Listen, Emma,' Sarah said, sitting down on a stool and taking hold of both of Emma's hands, 'I want you to promise me something.'

Emma knew by the look on her mother's face that this was something important, so she nodded in agreement.

'Will you be sure to tell me if Gamboo ever says she wants anything?'

Emma was puzzled but she promised that she would tell her mother; and then she said, 'But what sort of things do you mean? If Gamboo wants anything she usually goes to the shops herself and gets it.'

Sarah gave a sigh and looked out of the kitchen window where she could see the covered way and the patio. The plants in the tubs and hanging baskets were coming to the end of their flowering period and would soon need to be taken out and tidied up, she realised.

'It's difficult to say what I mean sometimes,' she smiled at Emma, '. . . but for instance, Gamboo hasn't mentioned those hanging baskets but before she does do you think you could take them down for her? We don't want her wobbling about on step ladders, do we?'

'Oh, is that all,' Emma said feeling relieved. 'Yes of course I'll do them. Gamboo might have one of her dizzy spells and it would be terrible if she fell off. Shall I do them now?'

'Yes, please, love, that would be kind of you. What dizzy spells are these? She hasn't said anything to me about that,' Mother said.

Emma paused with her hand on the door handle and looked back at her mother. 'It's several weeks ago that it happened. Gamboo had a dizzy spell, lost her balance and tumbled into the broom cupboard. She didn't hurt herself; it wasn't a fall . . . just a tumble.'

Sarah said nothing and Emma didn't see the tears glistening in her mother's eyes.

7

Paul was late for the evening meal once again. He'd spent the entire afternoon down at the swimming baths improving his butterfly stroke and had lost track of the time.

'Sorry,' he said, slithering into his seat.

'We'll forgive you, thousands wouldn't,' Alan said amiably.

'After all it is your holiday and we don't have to keep to a school timetable,' Sarah said, serving out a large portion of chicken curry and rice.

'Thanks, Mum, and you could sure give refectory a few lessons in cookery. This smells delicious,' said Paul, gratefully accepting his plate.

Alan looked around the table to see if everyone had what they wanted. Then he asked, 'Whose turn is it to say grace?'

'Mine,' Emma said and then continued with closed eyes, 'May food and friendship keep us strong, may love and laughter feed us. Amen.'

When everyone had started eating Dad said quietly to Emma, 'That was a nice thought. Where did you find it? In one of your books?'

'No, I made it up,' she replied. 'Most people thank God for their food but I think other things make us grow too.'

Alan smiled and slowly repeated, '. . . laughter, love and friendship . . . yes, that's another sort of food, you're quite right.'

The conversation moved in a general zig-zag way between the four of them for a while until a quiet period descended. Paul broke the silence by saying, 'When are you taking your fortnight's holiday, Dad? And where are we going this year?'

'Ah, well now.' Dad paused a moment and looked across at Sarah. 'I'm only taking a week this time and your mother and I decided that it might be better just to spend days out – visit places by car . . . that sort of thing.'

Paul simply raised his eyebrows slightly and said, 'Oh, I see. Yes, that sounds fine.'

Emma looked from one to the other and then across at her mother. This was the first time that the family wouldn't be having a holiday away somewhere. Some years it had been kept a secret from Paul and Emma until the very last minute but that had only made the surprise better when they did find out. But this was a huge disappointment and it puzzled Emma that Paul seemed to take it so calmly. She was just opening her mouth to ask why they weren't going on holiday when she felt something dig into her leg. It was the toe of Paul's shoe and when she looked up at him he fixed her with a meaningful stare that quite obviously said, 'Be quiet'.

'Have you decided on any places to visit or are you open to suggestions?' Paul enquired.

Alan poured himself a glass of water and took a long drink.

'Suggestions are welcome so long as it's something we can all enjoy.'

'Hear, hear,' Sarah laughed. 'Gamboo and I do not

intend to go pot-holing or abseiling just to please you.'

Paul grinned and shook his head, 'No, nothing like that, but how would it be if we went to Valorium?'

'Absolutely, I'll have three dozen of those,' teased Dad.

As Mother tidied away the plates she stood for a moment looking thoughtful. 'Now I've remembered. I knew I'd heard the name before . . . it's that Roman villa that they've begun to excavate.'

'That's right Mum, and it's only about forty miles north of here. Actually they've been digging for a few years now so there's really quite a lot to see.'

Emma listened without making any comment. She was not impressed with the idea. Firstly she knew nothing about the Romans and secondly she didn't think that a place where people were digging sounded much fun for a day out.

Afterwards, when they were alone, she rounded on Paul sharply and said, 'Why did you kick me under the table like that?'

'Because I wanted you to think before you spoke. OK so we don't get a holiday away this time . . . but they have their reasons if you stop to think about it.'

Emma felt confused. What reason could there possibly be for not having a holiday? They'd always had one. Every summer that she could remember they'd been somewhere but now suddenly Mum and Dad had decided against it without a word to anyone. It simply wasn't fair. The corners of her mouth turned down and she began to feel more and more rebellious.

'What reasons then? I can't think of any,' she said, striding along the landing toward her own room. Paul put out an arm and barred her way.

'Don't be so grumpy, Emma. Hasn't it occurred to you that turning the old games room into a flat must have cost a lot of money? And holidays are expensive, you know.'

'But Gamboo paid for the alterations, didn't she?' Emma said quickly.

'Well, she could only pay half,' Paul replied.

No more was said on the subject and when Emma was alone in her room she began to think about what Paul had told her. She'd never stopped to think about how much a holiday for their whole family must cost Dad and Mum. She'd always just taken it for granted. She felt rather ashamed.

Also it was a bit frightening to realise how quickly that selfish part of herself could take over: one minute she'd been saying grace, thanking God for all his gifts, and within a very few minutes she'd turned into a selfish, grumpy person who'd forgotten how to be grateful to her own mum and dad. Emma looked in the mirror and could still see traces of her cross, it's-not-fair face with downward curving lips and frown lines on her forehead.

'Get lost, Greta Grotbox,' she said severely to the mirror image, and then she replaced it with a smiling-Emma face instead.

On Sunday morning, when Emma was on her way round to see Gamboo, she noticed that the curtains were still drawn. Usually she was up and about long before Emma and so this was a little worrying. After breakfast the curtains were still not opened and when Dad and Paul went off to church Emma and her mother waited, wondering what to do.

It wasn't until nearly ten o'clock that Gamboo buzzed: Sarah picked up the phone immediately and Emma stood listening to half the conversation.

'Yes, we wondered if we ought to come round and see,' said Sarah.

There followed a long explanation from Gamboo to

which Sarah replied, 'Oh, I am sorry. Yes, I think I've got some . . . I'll send Emma round with them.'

Her mother opened the first-aid box and removed a packet of pain killers which Emma took round to the flat. Gamboo was still in her dressing gown when she opened the door.

'Are you all right, Gamboo?' Emma said.

Gamboo held out her hand for the tablets and then said wearily, 'It feels as though there's a little man with a hammer inside my head and he's trying to bang his way out.' She gave a weak smile.

'I know, headaches are horrid,' Emma said sympathetically, '. . . but those tablets should do the trick.'

'I certainly hope so,' Gamboo sighed.

'Is there anything I can do for you? Shall I make your breakfast?'

'No thanks my dear, not now. I'm going back to bed for a while . . . but perhaps a poached egg later.'

Emma went back and told her mother that Gamboo was staying in bed, and she mentioned about the poached egg too. It was agreed that Mother would see to that because Emma had previously arranged to go to Anita's for Sunday lunch.

By the time Emma returned Gamboo was up and the headache was a little better but even so she still looked very tired.

'I think perhaps you'd better go to church without me just this once,' Gamboo said in answer to Emma's question.

It was very unlike Gamboo to miss church and it seemed very strange to be going without her. Once in church her absence was even more obvious; the empty space in the pew beside Mother and no deep, rich voice adding its strength to each hymn. Over the months Gamboo had moderated the volume somewhat but even so her voice could still be heard clearly.

That day Emma said a silent prayer to Jesus asking for Gamboo not to have such bad headaches.

The next day Gamboo did feel much better and by Wednesday she was her usual lively self again. Wednesday was the day they'd chosen for their visit to the excavation of the Roman villa and Emma had by now decided that she was interested after all; particularly since Paul had lent her one of his books about Roman life which was full of coloured illustrations.

The journey didn't take very long. They drove to the village of North Lullington, left the car there and walked the quarter of a mile to the site of the dig. Emma wasn't sure what she expected to see but a Roman villa sounded large and important. What she found when they got there were some sections of wall, a pile of stones, a few holes in the ground and several lengths of rope stretched between pegs. She decided that it would be wiser not to say 'Is this all?' even though that was her first reaction. Instead she picked her way along the path.

'How did they know that there was a Roman villa here to dig up?'

'Apparently a local farmer was ploughing one of his fields,' Paul explained, '. . . and some tessera came to the surface of the soil.'

'Did they?' Emma exclaimed and then, linking arms with Gamboo, she whispered 'What are *they*?'

'Little tiles from a mosaic,' Gamboo whispered back, winking at Emma.

A short way ahead they came to a quite deeply sunken area and there lay the remains of a mosaic floor. Tiny blue, brown and white tiles had once formed an intricate pattern of which only fragments were left.

'This is better. You can almost see what it used to be like,' said Emma.

Sarah was gazing at it too and then she said, 'Think of all the feet that must have walked across that floor; I wonder what sort of things were important in their lives.'

'Very much the same as is important in ours I should imagine,' said Gamboo. 'Homes and families and what they believed in, and the work they had to do.'

Emma was still thinking of Roman feet walking across the mosaic floor: some in sandals and some in ankle length leather boots. She also remembered some of the pictures in the book Paul had lent her . . . the Roman men had worn short tunics for everyday wear and flowing togas for special occasions, and the women had floated about in thin gauzy dresses with their hair piled up on their heads or falling in graceful ringlets. In her daydream she pictured them gliding across this mosaic floor and talking to each other – in Latin she supposed. A sudden cool breeze swirled around them, bringing Emma out of her daydream and making Gamboo pull her jacket more closely around her.

'That had an autumn chill about it,' said Gamboo.

'I was just thinking,' said Emma, 'wouldn't the Romans have been cold over here in this country? It's not sunny like Italy.'

Gamboo smiled. 'They weren't all foreigners you know. Many of them were born in Britain and whereas the educated ones understood Latin the majority of Roman Britains probably spoke their own dialect.'

Paul had come along the path behind them and, overhearing the conversation, he said, 'You were talking about them feeling cold, Emma. Don't forget they would have had a hypocaust in a villa this size.'

'Oh yes, of course. It mentioned that in your book,' Emma said. For a little while everybody moved around the roped-off sections looking for a signpost that said Hypocaust. It was Sarah who found it.

'Look, can you see over there, a few of those hollow bricks are still in position,' she said.

Emma bent over the edge of the trench to get a better view. This was the area that was being excavated at the moment and although nobody was working there that day, there were the spoil heaps visible at the far end of the trench.

'They had a furnace that heated air and sent it through those hollow bricks under the floor,' said Emma, remembering the explanation in the book.

'Perhaps they'll find traces of the furnace when they've dug a little further along,' said Sarah.

Alan suddenly called out to them from the other side of the site.

'Come and look at this.' He was reading from a free information leaflet lying beside a notice saying Please Take One. 'This tells us more about Villa Valorium. Apparently it was the home of a Christian family and they've found the remains of a small family chapel.

'But I thought the Romans were horrid to the Christians,' said Emma.

'Some were, but not all,' Gamboo said softly.

Sarah had joined Alan and together they were reading from the information sheet. 'It says that over there was the find-spot of some silver articles,' she said, pointing to a small roped-off area. 'And one or two of the plates and goblets were from the period around AD 97. Think of that, Emma, only about a hundred years after Christ was on earth.'

Gamboo took up the story saying, 'Many of the citizens of Rome heard the news about Jesus in those early days and they believed that to follow his teachings was the best way to live.'

'So really it's because of the Romans that Britain heard about Jesus. I'd never thought of it like that before,'

Emma said.

'Not all Romans followed Christ's teachings. A great many still believed in their former gods. It wasn't until much later that Christianity became the state religion of Rome,' Gamboo said.

Paul came back to where the rest of the family was standing and he looked from one to the other. 'Well, have you enjoyed today? I certainly have, but I'm getting hungry. How about you?'

There were murmurs of agreement from Gamboo, Sarah and Alan but Emma still had that far-away look in her eyes. Her body stood there amongst the stone ruins and the turned earth but her thoughts were back hundreds of years in the past.

'I wish I could have met them,' she said dreamily.

'And I wish their hypocaust was still working,' said Gamboo, making her point even more strongly by letting her teeth chatter.

Paul immediately pulled off his jacket and draped it over her shoulders for added warmth. Gamboo smiled and thanked him.

'Let's head back to the village,' said Alan, 'I think I saw a little tea shop down one of the side streets.'

'A cup of tea would just round off the afternoon nicely,' Sarah said, '. . . and perhaps a toasted teacake as well.'

'Dripping with butter,' Emma added as she linked arms with Paul and set off along the path towards the village.

They had several other family outings after that, all interesting and all different. Sometimes it was just the York family and Gamboo and other times either Lauren or Anita would go with them, although that did make for rather a squash in the car, but nobody minded.

All too soon the summer ended and for Paul and

Emma school beckoned. With the autumn term would come harvest festival and after that bonfire night, so there was plenty to look forward to even though the evenings were lengthening. And then the old year would end with the festival of Christmas telling the story of the nativity to bring joy and hope for yet another year.

But before that came the time for saying goodbye to Paul for another term. On his last day at home Paul went round to the flat to say goodbye to Gamboo and when he came back he was looking very serious and thoughtful. He had something clasped in his hand.

'What have you got there?' Emma asked.

'A little present from Gamboo,' he replied.

Paul opened his hand and lying across his palm was a small ivory crocodile carved so delicately and in such detail that even the tiny teeth were clearly visible. He ran his fingers across the ivory figure and smiled.

'Weeks ago I happened to say that I thought this little creature was beautifully ugly . . . which seemed to amuse Gamboo . . . and now she's just given it to me.' He paused for a moment and then added, 'I didn't ask for it, you understand, she just said would I look after it for her.'

Emma looked up at her brother and then smiled, remembering a time several months previously when something very similar had happened to her.

'Gamboo sometimes does that. She handed me some mother-of-pearl buttons one day and asked if I liked them. Then she said I could have them because she wouldn't be needing them any more.'

Paul opened his suitcase and carefully tucked the ivory crocodile down safely amongst his clothes. The taxi would soon be coming to take him to the station. He didn't want any family waiting on the station platform, he preferred to say his goodbyes at home. There was a last minute hustle and bustle, kisses and hugs and then Paul got into the taxi but before he went he said to his mother, 'You can always phone our house master if you need me.'

Emma heard what he'd just said to Mother but at the time she didn't attach any importance to the remark. It was to be many weeks before she understood why Paul had said it.

The beginning of the new term and her twelfth birthday happened on the same day, so it was a busy day for Emma. For the early evening Mother had arranged a Splash Party at the swimming baths in town. Everyone swam until they were hungry and then sat at little tables to eat egg or chicken and chips, followed by birthday cake and hot chocolate. After a suitable period of time Emma and most of her friends pulled their soggy swim suits on again and went for a last half hour in the pool.

When the arrangements were being made the week before Gamboo had said she would happily join in with the eating but didn't think a dip in cold water was quite her style now. However, when the day actually arrived Gamboo said that she wasn't feeling very well and so she didn't go to the Splash Party after all.

'Can we take a piece of birthday cake home for Gamboo?' Emma said as she blew out the candles.

'Certainly, madam,' said the man when he came to pour out their hot chocolate, 'and we have boxes specially made for the purpose.'

At the end of the party Emma collected a small triangular box with a slice of cake inside and carried it safely home. Dad and Mother had had theirs at the pool side but Emma noticed that Dad had saved a few crumbs and a blob of icing for Puddy; strange food for a cat to enjoy.

There was only the dim glow of a table lamp showing

through Gamboo's curtains when Emma went round to the flat. She didn't see any movement in the room and, not wanting to disturb Gamboo if she'd fallen asleep, Emma went back into the house.

'Shall I leave the cake until tomorrow?' she said to her mother.

Sarah thought for a moment and then looked at her watch. It was nine o'clock. 'No, even if Gamboo is asleep now she won't want to spend all night upright in a chair. You can take it round later.'

Emma was quick to notice the word 'later'. How much later she wondered? It was already nearing her bedtime. When Dad came in from the garage where he'd been tinkering with the car, he washed his greasy hands under the tap.

'You still up?' he said giving Emma a wink. 'I suppose you've got a special dispensation.'

'Pardon?' said Emma.

'Extra time because it's your birthday.'

Emma grinned cheerfully, 'Yes, I'll go to bed soon but first I want to take this round to Gamboo,' she said, picking up the triangular cake box.

Dad dried his hands then reached up to the wooden rack that held the spice drawers. Inside one of the tiny drawers was the spare key to the flat. He handed it to Emma, 'Just in case she's in bed already,' he said.

'I won't make any noise,' she promised.

She tiptoed along the covered way making sure that her heels didn't clatter on the dark red quarry tiles. There was no lamp shining out now but there was still enough fading light to see where she was going. Emma turned the key in the lock and pushed open the door then quietly made her way to the kitchen.

At home she'd written a little note in case it was needed and she was just about to put it and the box of cake on the kitchen table when Gamboo called.

'Sarah, is that you? Come in here a minute, will you.'

Emma walked up to the bedroom door which was slightly ajar.

'It's not Mum, it's me. I came to bring you a piece of birthday cake.'

In the half light Emma could see that Gamboo was lying propped against a mound of white pillows. She smiled as Emma came in.

'That's kind of you. I'll enjoy that tomorrow.'

'Did you want Mum for something?' Emma asked.

'Not really, it'll do tomorrow. I'm sorry I missed your Splash Party.'

Emma sat on the edge of the bed and told Gamboo about her first day in a new class at school, and about some of the presents she'd been given for her birthday. As she was talking her hand went automatically to her new gold chain with its tiny golden cross which settled into the little hollow at her neck. This was her present from Gamboo.

'I really do like this. Thank you, Gamboo,' she said looking up into Gamboo's face.

Suddenly the old lady opened her eyes wide and gasped as a sharp, jagged pain stabbed inside her head. In the fast fading light Emma couldn't see the two tears that beaded from Gamboo's eyes, but she had heard the gasp and knew that something was wrong.

'What is it? What's the matter, Gamboo?' she asked.

There was silence for a few moments as Gamboo struggled to keep from crying out. She didn't want to frighten Emma, and she knew that the pain would pass as it had done many times before.

Eventually Gamboo managed to speak. 'It's nothing dear, just my silly old head again. Could you get me some water please.'

Emma rushed into the kitchen, filled a glass with water and rushed back to the bedside. By now Gamboo had clicked on her reading lamp and was calmly waiting with two little pink tablets cupped in her hand.

She took the water, swallowed the tablets and then smiled reassuringly at Emma. 'There we are. All gone,' she said.

'Are you sure you're all right? Shall I go and tell Mum?' Emma said anxiously.

'There's no cause to go worrying your mother. I shall be fine. Now then, say good night Jamie . . . and be a good boy.'

Emma looked startled. 'Gamboo . . . what do you mean? Why are you calling me Jamie? It's me . . . Emma.'

Gamboo looked at her closely for a moment or two then laughed rather harshly. 'I never did . . . did I?' Emma nodded. 'How stupid of me, of course you're not Jamie; but you looked like him in the half light.'

'Who is Jamie?' asked Emma.

'Jamie was my little boy . . . but he grew up,' Gamboo sighed heavily. 'Never mind, all that was a long time ago. Say goodnight now, dear.'

Emma bent over and kissed Gamboo then, as the little light went out, she quietly slipped out of the front door, clicking it shut behind her. Once back in her own kitchen she replaced the spare key in the spice drawer and then got a drink of water for herself. Remembering what Gamboo had said, Emma didn't go into any details about the headache or about having been called Jamie: she just said that Gamboo was awake and had thanked her for the cake. Then she said goodnight and went up to bed.

Upstairs in her own room she began to get ready for bed but she was feeling very uncomfortable; she'd had a happy birthday and everything should have been wonderful . . . but it wasn't. Something was wrong, she could feel it.

Thoughts raced round in her head but she couldn't pin them down long enough to make any sense out of them. There was something so strange about Gamboo in those few seconds when she'd talked about Jamie . . . as if it was a different person and not the Gamboo she knew. It was almost frightening.

Something was happening that she didn't understand but she could sense that it was important. Emma felt very uneasy.

It was hard to get rid of an uneasy feeling that didn't make any sense to her but she tried to say her prayers as usual.

Even after she'd said her prayers she still felt unsettled . . . and a bit cross that her birthday was having a peculiar ending. But a thought like that only made things worse. So she tried to ask Jesus the question that kept on coming back into her mind.

'Why did Gamboo mistake me for a little boy called Jamie? It wasn't just because the room was dimly lit . . . was it?'

Her question remained unanswered and after a long time of tossing and turning she eventually fell asleep.

8

The sound of the wind shrieking through the letter box made the morning seem even colder than it really was. Emma took one look at the way the trees were bending against the force of the wind and decided against riding her bicycle to school. It would be difficult to remain upright. Dad would drop her off on his way to work and even though it meant she would be at school half an hour early Emma knew that it was better than struggling there on her bike.

She hurried with her breakfast and was ready well before her dad so she wandered into the kitchen where Mother was putting a bowl of cat food down for Puddy.

'Mum, I think there's something I ought to tell you.'

Mother looked up. 'What is it?'

'When I took the cake round last night Gamboo had one of those bad headaches again.'

Sarah didn't say anything, but just stood there looking into space, then in the next moment the cat flap rattled and Puddy arrived like a little grey whirlwind across the kitchen floor. This distraction allowed time for Sarah to consider what she was going to say to her daughter; and it also gave Emma a moment to think as well. Ought she to mention this strange business of Gamboo mistaking her for a boy called Jamie? Or wasn't it all that important anyway? She decided to keep it to herself for now.

At last Sarah spoke. 'I'm afraid Gamboo hasn't been feeling too well recently. It comes and goes. I'll go and see how she is later on.'

'Perhaps I can go in and talk to Gamboo when I get home from school if she's feeling better.'

'Perhaps,' said Mother.

A toot on the car horn brought the conversation to a halt, reminding Emma that Dad was ready to go.

It was an ordinary sort of day at school, nothing special happened and when four o'clock came Emma hurried along to the bus stop. There was nobody else waiting since most of the children caught the school bus which went in the other direction. Standing there in the bus shelter she watched the rubbish being swirled around by the wind and then left in a miserable little heap at the far end of the shelter. Then another sudden gust disturbed the little heap again and there, lying amongst the toffee papers and dead leaves, was a rainbow-coloured 'something'. At first Emma couldn't see what it was but when she bent closer she could see that it was a pencil. She picked it up and looked at it more closely; the lead was broken, the rubber at the end had been worn flat and it was streaked with mud. Whoever it belonged to hadn't taken much care of it and it had looked sad and unwanted lying there in the dirt. Emma felt she should rescue it; rainbow things are special and shouldn't be treated so badly. She dropped the pencil into her pocket intending to clean and sharpen it when she got home . . . but she forgot all about it so there it stayed, in the bottom of her pocket.

When Emma arrived home one of the first things she said to her mother was, 'How's Gamboo? Shall I go and see her?'

Mother was busy getting tea ready and didn't reply so, thinking that she hadn't heard, Emma repeated what she'd said. With a harassed look on her face Mother turned and stared at Emma before saying rather sharply, 'Don't worry at me now please. I've a lot on my mind,' and she began buttering the bread hastily, cutting each slice corner to corner with great determination.

Emma watched in silence. Even though her mother's remark hadn't been any sort of an answer to her question she could feel a tension in the air and decided that it would be wiser not to pursue the matter further.

She went upstairs and began doing her homework at the table in her bedroom. The window was open slightly and as she sat there working she heard Mother's footsteps tip-tapping across from their back door over to Gamboo's front door which was directly below Emma's dormer window.

When Gamboo had first arrived all those months ago she'd been surprised to find that Emma's room could be 'upstairs' in a bungalow since that seemed to be a contradiction in terms; however, because of the deep slope of the roof there was enough space for an upstairs at the back of the house. Gamboo had said that this was either a 'housalow' or a 'bunghouse'.

Because her window was slightly open Emma could hear the door opening and the sound of voices below; Gamboo was obviously up and about, Emma realised, and that must mean that she was feeling better. When Dad came home and tea was on the table Emma came downstairs; she was just in time to hear Mother say, '. . . so I've taken her something round on a tray.'

Then Dad said, 'And there's nothing more we can do, then?' Sarah shook her head.

'Can I go round after tea?' Emma asked.

Alan and Sarah both spoke at once, one saying not to disturb Gamboo now, and the other saying that she needed plenty of rest. But neither of them would tell

Emma what was the matter with Gamboo or how long she would be before she was better.

For the next four days the same sort of thing happened; Emma was at school all day of course but even when she was at home and might have seen Gamboo they wouldn't let her go round. She was presented with all kinds of excuses and reasons why this wasn't the right time to visit Gamboo. Emma couldn't understand why her parents were behaving like this; they were treating her like a child again and although they hadn't actually said 'Run away and play', they might just as well have done. It made her feel very cross.

Gamboo never treated her like a child. She would always talk to Emma as if she were adult which in turn made her feel and act more grown up. But if her parents were going to treat her like a child she might as well act like one. So she spent most of her time upstairs in her own room . . . sulking. It started as sulking but before long it was just a feeling of miserable bad temper, and yet she wouldn't allow herself to speak . . . even when they called upstairs to her.

On Saturday morning she crept downstairs, grabbed a bowl of cornflakes and a glass of milk to take upstairs and hurried back to her room because she didn't want to have to talk to anybody. It was while she was sitting in the window seat looking down at the back garden that she saw Dr Mills come in through the back gate. He rang Gamboo's bell and the door was opened for him. Emma sat there feeling even more depressed. He was a nice man . . . she often saw him down at the tennis club . . . but when he came to your house that was quite different. It meant illness.

About half an hour later the buzzer went and Emma knew that her mother had answered it because in the next few moments she was going into Gamboo's flat leaving the door open behind her.

Emma waited at the window feeling as though she were spying on them somehow, and then she realised that with the window closed she wasn't even being a good spy. She opened the window, watched and listened – then she heard Gamboo's voice quite clearly saying, 'Thank you, doctor, but I think I already knew that.'

A little later Sarah and Dr Mills came out, closed Gamboo's door and walked across the patio together towards the back gate.

'I'm afraid it happened sooner than we expected,' he said gravely.

'So do we just carry on as usual?' asked Sarah, sounding surprised.

Emma couldn't hear his reply because by now they were too far away. She couldn't make much sense out of the few remarks she'd heard but reason told her that it must be quite serious. It was time to put aside her stupid sulking and try to approach Dad and Mother again. She dashed downstairs and into the dining room but pulled up sharply because through the archway into the kitchen she could see her parents. Alan had his arms around Sarah and she had her head on his shoulder. This wasn't strange in itself, they often had a cuddle, but as Emma stood there she knew deep inside herself that both of them were upset about something. She was sure that it must be about the doctor's visit.

Alan was the first to notice Emma and he said, 'Hello love, have you had your breakfast?' Sarah moved out from between his arms and turned round. 'I didn't hear you come in,' she said.

Emma looked at both of them and then down at the carpet. Why talk about unimportant things? Why were they shutting her out and not telling her anything? Still staring at the patterns on the carpet she said very slowly,

'Did the doctor say when Gamboo will be better?'

'Oh, he just popped in to see how she was,' Mother said, trying to sound reassuring.

Emma knew that doctors didn't just 'pop in' unless someone had phoned for them . . . which meant that she wasn't exactly telling a lie . . . but very nearly.

'It's nothing for you to worry about, Emma,' said Dad, putting on that same soothing voice.

Emma could feel herself getting more and more irritated. Didn't they trust her . . . was that why they wouldn't tell her anything? Of course she was worried about Gamboo, and even more worried because there was all this secrecy. If Paul had been at home he'd have found out and then she could have asked him to tell her the truth.

'Fine,' said Emma in that sharp, clipped way that she'd copied from Paul. 'Then I'll go round and see for myself.' She brushed past her parents and headed towards the back door.

'No, Emma. Not now,' Dad said, and it was clear form his tone of voice that it would be wiser not to disobey.

Sarah stood in the middle of the kitchen looking first at her husband and then at her daughter who were both glaring at each other. She sighed.

'Emma, please don't be difficult . . . not just now. In a few days' time you can see Gamboo again, I promise.'

'OK, so I'm going out on my bike if no one objects to that.' Emma's mouth was drawn into a hard line and the toss of her head, making her red hair bounce, showed the extent of her displeasure.

'Take your coat then, it's cold out,' Dad called after her.

Riding along the rutted track down toward the farm she tried to think of all the possible reasons why they wouldn't let her see Gamboo; the worst one she could think of was that Gamboo might not want to see her. Surely that couldn't be the reason . . . Gamboo wasn't like that. When she came to Four Acre Field she got off her bike, propped it against the hedge and leant against the five bar gate, chewing the end of a sweet grass stem. In the distance she could see Fleet steadily cropping the grass, so she whistled; two ears swivelled round and when the old horse saw her he gave a loud whinny and came across to where Emma was waiting. She rubbed her hand lovingly across the hard brown cheek and looked deep into the dark eye that gazed back at her.

'What would you do if you were me?' she said solemnly. 'Do you think Gamboo would like to see me, or not?'

Fleet snorted noisily which could have been a 'yes' but was more likely to be his recognition of apple smells coming from Emma's pocket.

'I could go early tomorrow morning before Mum and Dad are up,' she confided, '. . . and wait for Gamboo to wake up. Then I could talk to her.'

The old horse bobbed his head up and down several times as if agreeing with the idea. Emma smiled to herself and stroked his nose gently.

'That's what I'll do then,' she said, thrusting her hand into her pocket. The apple was there but so was something else. Emma gave Fleet his apple and then she pulled out the broken rainbow pencil which she had forgotten was there.

It was still broken and still dirty but at least living in her pocket was better than lying in the gutter. 'I'll sort you out when I get home,' she said, replacing it in her pocket.

For the rest of the day Emma was very quiet and kept

well out of the way. Now that she'd decided what she was going to do in the morning she felt she could keep the secret better if no one looked into her eyes. Dad had a habit of saying 'Look into my eyes and tell me . . .' if he thought there was some doubt about the truth . . . and Emma couldn't risk her plan being discovered.

During the evening Sarah popped her head round the door of Emma's bedroom and said, 'Are you all right? You've been up here most of the day all by yourself.'

Emma held up the rainbow pencil and showed it to her mother; the colours had been washed clean and the point was sharp again.

'I found it at the bus shelter, broken and messy, so I've done it up. That's not stealing, is it?' Emma said, just to be on the safe side.

'I hardly think so, it's more like finders keepers . . . unless you want to put a card in the post office window saying "Will the owner of a scruffy pencil with a flattened rubber please contact Emma York" . . . Someone *might* phone you.'

'You're not serious?' said Emma.

'No, I'm not serious,' her mother laughed. 'Now, why don't you come down and have some supper.'

When she went to bed Emma had tucked her digital alarm under her pillow so that the beep-beep would wake her but nobody else. Opening sleepy eyes she saw that it was twenty past six and barely light outside. Puddy lay curled at the bottom of the bed and took not the slightest notice as Emma crawled out of bed, pulled on her jogging pants and top and very quietly opened her door.

Being careful to avoid the third step from the top . . . the one that creaked . . . she crept downstairs and into the kitchen, then taking the spare key from the spice drawer she went outside into the misty morning air. The dew was still on the grass and here and there spider webs hung glistening from the bushes.

Once inside the flat Emma wondered if she had done something rather stupid after all; perhaps she'd get into serious trouble for coming when she'd been told not to. However, it was too late to worry about that now.

She sat at the kitchen table and waited for what seemed to be a very long time before there were any sounds from the bedroom; but now Gamboo was obviously getting up so Emma plugged in the kettle. To find a cup of tea ready would be a nice surprise for Gamboo, she thought.

It was in fact Emma who got the surprise because when Gamboo came into the kitchen her head and both hands were swathed in bandages. Emma gasped and ran across to her.

'Whatever has happened to you?' she cried out.

Gamboo sat down at the table with her back to the window and said, 'I fell over while I was carrying a tray full of crockery, and cut myself on the broken pieces.'

'Poor you, is it very sore?'

'Not so bad, really, but I'll have to be a lot more careful in future.'

Seeing that the kettle was boiling Emma made a pot of tea and brought milk and sugar over to the table where two mugs were waiting.

'You're a good girl. What would I do without you?' said Gamboo, picking up the mug carefully between her bandaged hands.

Emma smiled. 'I *knew* it wasn't because you didn't want to see me . . . that's why I came.'

'What do you mean, dear?'

'It's Mum and Dad, they're making a big mystery out of everything and they wouldn't let me come and see you. I knew when I saw the doctor come that something had happened but they wouldn't tell me anything.'

Once Emma began to talk she felt more and more sorry for herself and couldn't stop telling how badly she felt about being kept in the dark. 'They treat me as if I was a child . . . and I wanted to know because I love you just as much as they do . . . and I only wanted to know how long it'll be before you're better again.' Emma paused because she'd run out of breath but before she could set off again Gamboo stopped her.

'Emma, Emma . . . hush a minute and let me say something. Please let me try to explain first.'

Emma clasped her hands together tightly in an effort to prevent more words from coming bubbling out of her mouth.

Gamboo went on to say, 'Don't be so quick to blame your mother and father. Think of it from their point of view. They both love you very much and that's why they were trying to protect you . . . that's the only reason that they haven't answered your questions.'

'Protect me from what? I'm not frightened by a few bandages.'

Gamboo raised her bandaged hands in front of her and looked at them.

'These will soon heal . . . But, let's go and sit in the other room where it's more comfortable.'

By this time the morning sun was shining through the last wisps of mist and Emma ran ahead into the living room. With one hand she pulled back the curtain but as a shaft of sunlight blazed into the room Gamboo stepped back, raising one arm to shield her eyes.

'Please . . . close the curtain. The bright glare is hurting my eyes.'

Emma did as she was asked and then came to sit near Gamboo on the sofa. It seemed very odd to be shutting out the sunlight. Gamboo usually loved sunshine.

'It's sometimes hard for parents to realise that their

children are almost grown up.' Gamboo patted Emma's hand gently before continuing. 'However, I'm not going to treat you like a child; I think it is something you should be told and I'm the best person to tell you. My headaches and dizzy spells, and now falling over and finding bright light painful . . . these are all part of an illness I've got.'

'Oh I see, and so the doctor is treating you for that. How long will it be before you're better?'

Gamboo just shook her head.

'He hasn't told you how long? Why is that, doesn't he know?'

'No one can say for sure . . . such things are in God's hands, not ours.'

Emma didn't quite know why but she began to feel a bit uncomfortable about this conversation. She remembered hearing the doctor talking to Mother on the patio . . . what was it he had said though? She couldn't remember his actual words.

'Look at me,' said Gamboo. 'You can't see because of the bandages but I'm smiling underneath; try to remember that. I'm an old lady, I've been around a long time and I can't last forever you know. But I can smile inside because I know everything will be all right at the end.'

'The end . . . of what?' Emma said rather shakily because she was on the very edge of understanding what Gamboo meant.

'The end of my life . . . we all have to face that truth sooner or later, and in a way it's something very wonderful to look forward to; don't you think so?'

'No, I do not,' said Emma very definitely, '. . . not when it's someone you love. Anyway I don't want to think about it even.' There were tears in her eyes as she looked up at Gamboo.

'Emma, you wanted me to treat you like an adult and

so I've told you what your mother and father didn't feel able to tell you. Now it's up to you to be a big strong girl and accept what must come. I know that before very much longer I shall be meeting my saviour and my friend, Jesus Christ. Can't you be happy for me?'

'But Gamboo, I don't want you to die, it frightens me to think of it. What if it isn't true . . . any of it? What if when you die there isn't anything afterwards? Donald at school says you just get put in a box and that's the end of it,' Emma said with a tremble in her voice.

Gamboo got up and went over to the cupboard. She took out a black velvet pouch and then came back to the sofa. Emma sat watching and wondering what was inside the little pouch which Gamboo had placed on the cushion beside her.

'Well, I happen to think that Donald Whoever-he-is has got it all wrong, but each person has to make up their own mind about the things they believe in. We mustn't force our ideas onto other people; they have to discover for themselves what they believe is the truth. All I know is that for me the promise that Jesus made feels right and true: he came to tell us that life is everlasting and that it is only this outer body that dies.'

Emma took a deep breath and let it out very slowly. She wasn't sure what she believed at this very moment, the thoughts were very big and she felt very small. Even if she tried to reason it out it didn't make any sense . . . and Donald's doubts still clouded her mind.

Gamboo was sitting quietly watching, leaving Emma all the time she needed, and hoping that telling her the truth about the illness hadn't been a mistake after all.

At last Emma looked up. 'If Jesus is your friend why does he let you be ill at all? That doesn't sound like friendship to me.'

'These things are difficult to understand but we just

have to trust, and we have to accept,' said Gamboo.

'No,' said Emma fiercely, 'I can't just accept; it isn't fair to make people suffer pain and illness. That's not a nice way for God to run the universe if he's supposed to be loving.'

Gamboo began to chuckle which Emma thought was rather strange of her.

'What's funny about that?' said Emma.

'If you don't like the way the universe is being run you'll have to complain to the management later. I wonder if God has a suggestion box in heaven?'

'Oh Gamboo, how can you joke about it?'

'Because laughter is a better medicine than anything you can buy at the chemist.'

Emma attempted a weak little smile but before she'd thought what to say next Gamboo pointed to the velvet pouch beside her on the cushion.

'Will you open it for me? My fumbly fingers can't work inside all these bandages.'

Emma picked up the pouch and pulled open the drawstring. Inside was what seemed to be a flat oval box that shimmered with all the colours of the rainbow.

'It's beautiful. What is this?'

'They made it from the inside part of an abalone shell which they call mother-of-pearl. Do you see a little notch at one side? Open it up with your finger nail.'

Emma prised apart the two hinged ovals and there inside were two small photos: one of Gamboo and the other obviously of Great-Grandad.

'These photos were taken three years before he died,' Gamboo said, taking the photo frame and gazing back at the two smiling faces. 'And I'm really looking forward to meeting him again. Can you understand how I feel?'

Emma felt a lump come in her throat and she swallowed hard to prevent tears from coming. 'Yes Gamboo,

I can understand . . . but I still don't want you to leave us.'

'Well, I've not got my bags packed and I'm not going just yet awhile, so don't look so miserable. You'll turn the milk sour.' Gamboo laughed and then clicked the mother-of-pearl frame shut again. She fumbled with the velvet pouch, forgetting her bandaged fingers.

'I'll do it for you,' said Emma.

'Good girl. Actually Dr Mills told me the bandages can come off soon.'

As Emma replaced the photo frame in its pouch she suddenly said, 'It's like a rainbow, isn't it? I collect rainbow things too. I've got a badge I bought at Roundel Woods and a pencil I rescued from a bus shelter. Rainbows are special I think.'

'Yes indeed,' said Gamboo, '. . . very special.'

9

In the evening of that same day Gamboo buzzed and when Sarah answered Gamboo asked for Emma to go round. She rushed next door wondering if everything was all right but found Gamboo happily sitting with a pencil and paper on her lap.

'Two reasons for asking for you,' she said cheerfully. 'One, will you write the order for half a dozen eggs as well as a pint of milk. And two, do you want me to tell your mother and father that you know . . . about me?'

'Oh yes, please, Gamboo, that would make it easier,' Emma said with relief, 'I didn't quite know how I was going to get round that difficulty.'

'Leave it to me, then,' Gamboo said quietly, '. . . and put that note in the milk bottle on your way out. Goodnight, dear.'

The weekend came and with it came the doctor to remove Gamboo's bandages. She had one rather black eye but that soon vanished and the cuts on her hands had healed wonderfully.

Emma tried over the next few weeks to accept the idea of Gamboo only having a short time to live, but she found it almost impossible. At first she really did try to pray and her prayers always asked for the same thing, 'Please make Gamboo better'. But it didn't seem that

God was listening because as time went by Gamboo began to get weaker. The change was only slight at first but it was obvious to Emma because she was watching for it. At least now that there wasn't that secrecy Emma could talk openly to her mother and father which made life less tense. The three of them worked out a timetable between them so that there was always somebody available to go round to the flat when Gamboo buzzed.

However there was still one big problem that Emma couldn't find a way to solve. She knew that Gamboo had placed all her trust in Jesus and yet Emma herself felt a growing anger which she couldn't even talk to Gamboo about. Beforehand Gamboo had always been so good at helping Emma to solve her problems, but now that had gone. When Sundays came round Emma began to feel very uncomfortable about going to church; Dad still went twice because of the choir and Mother usually went in the evening, but Emma began finding all sorts of excuses why she couldn't go with them.

And then came that Sunday in November when everybody wore poppies. Gamboo had really wanted to go to that service and so Sarah had helped her to dress and Emma had even found a pair of dark glasses to protect her eyes from the light. With Sarah supporting her on one side and Alan on the other Gamboo had walked down the aisle to sit near the front.

Emma sat watching this thin, frail old lady making such an effort to be in church, then she remembered how tall and strong Gamboo had once been . . . and suddenly a rage boiled up inside Emma that was so furious that she could hardly bear to remain sitting down. How could Jesus let this happen to her dear Gamboo? Someone who all her life had believed and trusted . . . it was both unkind and unjust. Only the fact that she didn't want to cause a scene prevented

Emma from getting up and walking out of church that very moment.

Emma didn't go to any more services after that. Alan tried to find out why but Sarah had already guessed what was the matter and persuaded him not to make an issue of it.

At school Emma was finding it difficult to concentrate on her work. Her mind kept returning to the situation at home and, compared with what was happening there, maths and French seemed rather unimportant.

'What's bothering you?' Lauren said one day. 'You're not with us, are you? Your body may be here but your head is miles away.'

'Let's call her Longfellow then,' Anita said, laughing loudly at her own joke.

'Leave me alone, will you. I don't want to talk,' Emma said, walking away, but Lauren followed her into the cloakroom.

'Come on, you can tell us what*ever* it is; we're your friends.'

Emma held on to one of the coat pegs and let her head hang forward until her face was hidden behind a curtain of hair. There was silence for several moments, then in a muffled voice she said, 'It's Gamboo.'

Once she started the whole story came flooding out and afterwards she admitted that it was a great relief to have been able to tell them.

Anita put her arms round her and Lauren offered a large hanky to mop up the tears.

'I wonder what it *is* like when you get to heaven?' Anita said brightly, trying to think of something comforting, '. . . I don't go for the angels-with-harps idea but I'd like there to be something waiting for us . . . beautiful and happy and all that.'

'Perhaps it'll be somewhere where you can do all the

things you weren't able to do on earth,' said Lauren, '. . . like a new chance to be yourself, but to do it better.'

Emma looked at her friends and wished she still had their optimism.

'I don't even know if I believe in heaven anymore. Nobody really knows, do they?'

'Does Gamboo think there's a heaven?' said Anita.

'Yes, and she expects to meet Great-Grandad there. I hope there is for her sake because she's getting a pretty rotten deal down here on earth,' said Emma sadly.

Gradually, as the weeks passed, Emma spent more and more of her free time with Gamboo. In a strange way she almost began to enjoy the feeling of doing little jobs around the flat, dusting and keeping things tidy; it was almost as though she was keeping house . . . But then suddenly she'd feel guilty because that meant she'd forgotten why she was here. The reason would then make her feel sad . . . soon Gamboo would need her help more and more. All those months ago when Gamboo was fit and strong she'd been the one who helped Emma . . . to draw, to make things, to understand things . . . but now the roles were reversed and it was Emma who had to be the strong one. Of course Mother was always there to help with the practical things, but Emma found it hard to accept that her special relationship with Gamboo was changing. And yet Gamboo still had that strange sense of humour which Emma had grown to appreciate, and she could make Emma laugh sometimes at the silliest little things. Occasionally Gamboo would say something that didn't seem to make sense to Emma but she tried not to look too surprised.

However, one evening something happened which Emma found quite frightening. She had let herself into the flat and found Gamboo standing staring out of the window. In the half light Emma couldn't see what

Gamboo was looking at.

'What is it Gamboo? What can you see?' she said.

Gamboo turned round and in a very stern voice she said to Emma, 'I'll tell you what I can see . . . a mess. Look at that garden, it's a disgrace, leaves and rubbish blown everywhere. Go and tell that lazy kabun that I pay him to keep this place tidy. Go on, bring him to me.'

Emma couldn't believe what she was hearing nor could she understand what Gamboo was talking about but there was such authority in that voice that it made Emma jump. She just looked helplessly at Gamboo.

'Don't stand there with your mouth open, girl, do as I ask. And while I think of it, as Jamie's amah you really shouldn't have let him wander away like that all by himself. Please don't let it happen again.'

Gamboo turned on her heel and with a wave of dismissal she walked away. Emma only stayed long enough to make sure that Gamboo had settled herself safely on the sofa, and then she dashed back home. Mother was in the kitchen.

'What's happened? You look terrified.'

'Gamboo shouted at me . . . well, perhaps not shouted exactly, but it made me feel awful, as if I'd done something wrong.

'What did she say to you?'

'She called somebody a lazy cabin and told me I was Jamie's arm . . . or some funny word like that . . . it didn't make any sense.'

Sarah looked thoughtful as she turned the gas out under the saucepan.

'She mentioned Jamie? Then she must have been thinking about Malaysia a long time ago.' She paused and moved the saucepan off the stove. 'That was my Uncle James she was talking about, and she thought you were the amah . . . that's like a nanny or housekeeper.'

'What did the other funny word mean?' asked Emma.

'Do you remember the man in the photo . . . holding a rake? He was a kabun, it just means a gardener.'

'What makes her talk like that? It's as though she was somebody else, not the Gamboo I know.'

'Did you call her Gamboo?'

'Yes, of course, I always call her Gamboo,' said Emma, surprised.

'That could account for it. That was the name she was known by on the plantation in Malaysia; in her mind she was back there in the old days. Old people often find that their early memories are clearer than what's happening in the present . . . and they get confused.'

Sarah untied her apron and hung it on the hook behind the door.

'I'd better go and see that she's all right. Are you coming with me?'

Emma hesitated for a moment but then she said yes. Together they went into the flat and turned on a dim light. Gamboo looked up as they came in and she smiled.

'I think I've been asleep,' she said mildly, '. . . it was quite a surprise to wake up and find myself here.'

'Have you been dreaming about Malaysia?' Mother asked.

'Yes, I have, but how could you possibly guess that?' Gamboo smiled sweetly at them both, the remarks of the past quite forgotten.

After that Emma got used to Gamboo saying things that didn't belong to here and now, and she even found herself having to explain this to Robert Timms one day when he stopped her in the village street.

Recently he'd been coming to the flat to share the Communion bread and wine with Gamboo and apparently after the little service she'd said it was good to have a service taken by a real minister for a change. Robert had been puzzled but hadn't asked her what she meant. However he'd been curious enough to ask Emma about it later.

'It was the expression "a real minister" that confused me,' he said, '. . . and Mrs Gimbourne addressed me as Ralph. A case of mistaken identity.'

Emma smiled. 'I don't know who Ralph was but I do know that Great-Grandad built a tiny church for the employees on his land, and so I suppose he was the one who usually took the services.'

'Yes, that would explain it.' Then changing the subject he added, 'We've missed you in church; you haven't been for a long time have you . . . but I expect you are being a great help to your great-grandmother.'

Emma breathed a sigh of relief; she didn't think she could tell him the real reason just now, so she was thankful for his assumption.

'I hope so,' she said demurely.

Christmas was approaching and this brought Emma very mixed feelings. The good things were that Paul would soon be home again and the family always had a wonderful time at Christmas . . . but on the other hand the very mention of the Nativity forced her to face her own inner problem. How could she sing or even listen to carols about the birth of Jesus when in her own sad heart she was blaming him for not healing Gamboo? If Jesus could make the blind see and the lame walk in Palestine why was he doing nothing about Gamboo's illness? Emma felt wretched about the whole thing.

Sarah put the Christmas decorations up and Alan bought a real tree with roots so that it could spend the rest of its life in their garden instead of lying dismally on a rubbish tip after the festivities.

'Have you asked Gamboo if she wants some help with

the decorations?' said Mother.

'I could take round some holly and tinsel, and hang up her cards if you think she'd like that,' Emma replied.

'And can you still make that crib scene with all the animals that you used to cut out of white cardboard? It looked so pretty with candle light shining through the little spaces. I'm sure she'd like that,' Mother suggested.

Emma bit her lip. It seemed as though everything and everybody was pulling or pushing her towards thinking about the Christmas story . . . and she didn't really want to.

But she did hang some holly and tinsel in Gamboo's flat and the day after that she took cardboard, scissors and glue with her when she went round. When she explained about the little crib scene Gamboo seemed very pleased.

'That will be very festive, thank you dear; and I think I have a candle.'

Emma chattered on about this and that as she usually did when she was there, and when she mentioned that Paul was coming home Gamboo looked puzzled.

'Who's coming dear?'

'Paul . . . you remember . . . my brother Paul.'

'Oh, yes, I was there at his wedding, wasn't I? but I'm afraid I don't remember you,' she said sweetly. '. . . Where did we meet?'

A cold chill settled over Emma and she felt the sweat break out on the palms of her hands. It was someone else sitting in the chair . . . not her Gamboo, she was so distant and different.

'Gamboo, it's me . . . Emma,' she said tearfully, '. . . please remember me . . . oh, *please* Gamboo.'

By this time Gamboo had put on her polite face, the one she used when she met strangers, and she put out her right hand to shake hands with Emma.

'How do you do?' she said primly.

Emma ignored the offered hand, putting her arms around Gamboo instead and pressing her face so hard against the woolly cardigan that the imprint of a button was marked on her cheek. There must have been something about the holding and the close contact that brought Gamboo back to the present moment.

'Whatever are you crying about?' she asked suddenly.

Looking up into Gamboo's face now Emma saw the familiar merry twinkle in the eyes. Emma gulped and rubbed her squashed cheek.

'I thought you'd forgotten me,' Emma sniffed.

Gamboo looked down at her with great tenderness and just a trace of sad resignation, for she knew what the illness was doing to her mind.

'I'm so sorry if I upset you. It's this silly old brain of mine, it isn't working as well as it used to.'

Unfortunately these lapses of memory became more frequent and although being with Gamboo was something that Emma loved, her enjoyment was tinged with apprehension because she never quite knew what might happen next.

'Gamboo said that her brain isn't working properly; what did she mean? That's a frightening idea . . . what *is* happening to Gamboo?' Emma asked her mother one day.

Sarah put her arms around her daughter and hugged her. 'I know it's a difficult thing to understand but try not to worry. Inside she is still the same Gamboo we love but her brain is getting tired, that's all.'

'Your mother is right,' Alan said. 'Spirit never grows old but the body it has to live inside does.'

After Paul arrived home the feeling of Christmas holiday increased, mainly because he wouldn't allow Emma to dwell on the unhappy side of things. He jollied her out of her sad moods and kept her busy planning things to do. Together they went round to the flat and gave Gamboo hours of pleasure playing chess and mahjong or taking it in turns to read Gamboo's favourite passages from the Bible. There were an increasing number of times when Gamboo looked at Paul or Emma without recognising them: this still upset Emma very much and she didn't know how to react, but Paul always said the same thing to Gamboo . . . 'No problem, you'll remember in a minute . . .' and she did.

It was Paul's suggestion that they should hire a wheelchair now that Gamboo was finding it difficult to walk, and Sarah and Alan thought this was a brilliant idea. The day the chair arrived was sunny but very cold. However, Gamboo still said she would like to go out so they bundled her up in her warmest clothes, wound woolly scarves around her neck and tucked a big tartan travelling rug round her legs.

'Where do you want to go?' Paul asked.

'Just out, I don't mind where, but I want to get some fresh air in my lungs,' Gamboo replied.

Paul pushed the wheelchair out through the back gate and Emma closed the gate behind them. The back road went past three other bungalows and then turned right onto the road toward the village, but there was a grass track leading off to the left which led out beyond the golf course.

Paul looked at Emma and raised his eyebrows questioningly; she nodded. With two of them pushing it was fairly easy to manoeuvre the wheelchair over the bumps and hollows until they reached level ground again.

'Are you warm enough?' Emma asked.

'Yes, thank you dear.' Gamboo paused for a few moments before continuing. 'Look, isn't it beautiful? . . . the stark winter shape of trees silhouetted against that grey sky. All the leaves have gone . . . now they wait patiently for life to be reborn in the spring . . . just like I'm waiting.'

Neither Emma nor Paul said anything, because it was a difficult statement to comment upon. Gamboo turned her head and fixed Paul with her steady gaze.

'I wanted a last look before I go.'

Softly out of the cold sky were drifting the first flakes of snow. They settled like wisps of cotton wool on the grass and on their clothes.

'We'd all better go before this gets any thicker,' Paul said, but both he and Emma knew that this wasn't what Gamboo had meant.

Emma choked back a sob and Paul, putting his hand on her arm, gave a gentle squeeze of encouragement.

That evening Emma stayed up in her room feeling very depressed and eventually Paul knocked on her door. When he came in she tried to tell him how she was feeling but instead she burst into tears.

'Try not to be so upset about Gamboo,' he said.

'I can't help it. First she forgets who we are and then she says things that sound as though she *wants* to die and leave us. I wish it was all over.' Then Emma put her hand over her mouth in horror, 'No, I didn't mean that, honestly I really didn't mean it.'

Paul put his arm round her to comfort her. 'Listen, sis, don't be ashamed of what you just said . . . because that *is* what Gamboo is waiting for . . . for it all to be over.'

'But I don't want her to die, I want her to be like she used to be when I first knew her,' Emma sniffed.

'You know that that isn't going to happen, don't you? The Gamboo we know and love is still here but locked inside a body that is old and tired . . . a body that can't walk and a brain that forgets things. Gamboo's spirit is waiting to be free. So really we should be happy to let her go.'

It was strange to hear Paul saying almost exactly the same things that Mother and Dad has said when they'd been trying to comfort her and help her to understand. Emma struggled to accept this idea but she couldn't: half of her wanted to believe that Gamboo would be alive in some sort of heaven but the other half of her doubted that such a place even existed. All she was left with was a hollow emptiness that she couldn't find any way to fill.

Christmas Day arrived and the York family celebrated the event quietly. Emma tried very hard not to let the rest of the family see how hollow she felt but it was difficult. Gamboo was brought round in the wheelchair in time for Christmas dinner, they watched the Queen's speech on TV and Gamboo stayed until the early evening. Part of the time she was entirely with them and conscious of what was going on but the rest of the time she spent either reliving her past or nodding off to sleep.

Before she was taken back to her flat Gamboo took a lingering look at her family as if to imprint their faces on her fading memory, then she smiled.

'You have been very good to me and before I go I want to say thank you . . . all of you . . . for everything.'

Of course she could have been referring to Christmas Day, but there was such an air of finality about the way she said it that there were tears in everybody's eyes.

Emma went to see Gamboo on Boxing Day and found that she was feeling rather tired after the excitement of the day before and had stayed in bed.

'Can I get you anything? Do you want a drink or shall I read to you?'

Gamboo smiled but shook her head. Then she reached out and took Emma's hand. 'Just sit awhile and keep me company,' she said.

So Emma sat beside the bed in the dim light holding Gamboo's hand. The skin was so white that it almost looked transparent and she remembered again their first meeting, how straight and tall she had been, and how bronzed her skin then. All she could think of now was the unfairness of it all, that her dear Gamboo should have to live like this . . . ill and in pain.

She turned to look at the frail old lady lying propped against the pillows, and that was when she noticed that Gamboo was looking straight ahead with a strangely peaceful expression on her face.

Suddenly Gamboo squeezed Emma's hand and said almost in a whisper, 'Can you see him?'

'Who?' replied Emma.

Gamboo pointed at the Holman Hunt painting which hung on the wall opposite her bed. In the dim light Emma could hardly see any details but to Gamboo the painting had come alive.

'Jesus smiled at me,' she said softly. 'I saw it quite clearly a moment ago.'

Emma said nothing to break across the dream world that Gamboo was experiencing, but inside her own mind she said fiercely . . . 'Then why doesn't he *help* you?'

10

On the third of January Gamboo died peacefully in her bed. Even though the whole family had known that it must happen, the shock of her death affected each person in a different way. Alan and Sarah were very quiet and controlled and put all their energy into doing practical things like making arrangements and making numerous phone calls. Emma could see that her mother's eyes were often red-rimmed from crying, but then so were her own. She sobbed herself to sleep at night and wandered aimlessly about the house during the day because there wasn't anything for her to do. She did a lot of thinking, though.

Gamboo had been such an understanding person and such a close friend that at one point Emma had found herself half saying . . . 'If only Gamboo were here she'd help me through this awfulness . . .' and then, realising what she'd just said, it made her feel even more unhappy and deserted.

But Emma soon found how good it was to have a big brother like Paul, who always seemed to appear from nowhere just when he was needed most. He helped Mum and Dad with little jobs that no one had thought about . . . until they were done; and he helped Emma by accepting her misery and grief and not expecting her to hide it away.

There were many times when Sarah comforted her daughter and retold little things that she remembered about Gamboo's life in Malaysia. It was good still to be able to talk about Gamboo because in a strange way just mentioning her name made the unhappiness seem less overwhelming. Dad had a different way of comforting her: he would just rest his hand on her arm or give her shoulder a gentle squeeze and say, 'How's my girl?' Emma would always try to say, 'I'm all right', and then he'd reply, 'I do know how you feel.' And Emma was sure that he did know.

The snow was still spread across the countryside like a white blanket and the cold crisp air nearly took your breath away, but on the day before the funeral Paul said to Emma, 'Wrap up warmly and put your snow boots on, we're going out.'

'What for? I don't feel like going out.'

'Come on, I mean it. It'll do you good.'

Rather grudgingly she got herself ready and followed him outside. Their feet crunched on the re-frozen snow and their breath billowed out from their nostrils like clouds of steam. In silence they tramped along that same track that led toward the golf course but now the bumps and hollows over which they'd pushed Gamboo's wheelchair were evened out with a covering layer of deep snow.

'Why did you bring me here of all places?' Emma said bitterly.

'Because it's time to get rid of all that misery that's locked up inside you,' he told her.

'It's not just misery, it's anger as well: anger at Jesus and God and everything . . . because it's all so beastly,' she gulped and wiped her eyes with the back of her glove, '. . . and you are the only person I could say that to, I couldn't tell Mum and Dad.'

Emma knew that both her mother and father found help and comfort in what the church meant to them, and in a way she wished she still felt the same as they did. But Jesus hadn't listened to any of her prayers and so she'd just turned away from him . . . and now there didn't seem to be any way back.

Paul took hold of her hand. 'I know, and that's why I've brought you here.' He began running across the golf course and Emma scrambled to keep up with him.

Behind them appeared a double line of flurried footsteps marking their presence in an otherwise deserted landscape. At last Paul stopped running and they waited until both of them had got their breath back.

'Now, when I say one-two-three, you shout as hard as you can. There's no one here to hear us.'

'Do you mean . . . just yell?' asked Emma looking very surprised.

'Yes, as loud as you can, and put all your anger, misery and grief into one great enormous bellow . . . let it out of yourself and let it blow away into the sky.'

'Are you going to do it too?'

'You bet I am. So let's see who can yell the loudest.'

Emma took a deep breath and stood looking out across the white wilderness of the golf course; in her mind she collected up all her unhappiness and grief.

'One, two three . . . shout!' Paul cried out.

A great roar of sound escaped from their throats and went echoing through the frosty air . . . it reverberated in their own ear-drums like the waves of a storm sea crashing onto the rocks. After such a wall of sound the silence that followed seemed quieter than anything Emma had ever known. She flung her arms around her brother and hugged him, feeling exhausted but triumphant.

'Oh thank you Paul, what a great idea . . . and I

think it's really worked. I feel lighter, as if I'd thrown something heavy away.'

'Good, and I needed that shout as well,' he said.

'What made you think of doing it?' Emma asked.

'There's a lad called Jenkins in our dormitory and his father died last year. He told me that sometimes he used to walk along the cliff path and yell at the sea because he felt so screwed up and angry. I just thought it might help us . . . and wouldn't Gamboo have enjoyed *that* little exhibition?'

'Yes, I expect she would . . . if she could,' Emma said, her thoughts slipping back into sadness. 'Do you really think she's . . . somewhere?'

Paul pursed his lips and looked at her. 'I honestly don't know. But Gamboo believed it and she wasn't often wrong. However, it wouldn't be any help me saying what I believe and expecting you to accept it. Everyone finds their own way to understand.'

'Gamboo said that once too,' said Emma.

'You were lucky to have spent so much time with her; and I had to be away at school. That's something I feel sad about.'

They started back toward home, following their own earlier footprints in the snow. To Emma things now seemed a little brighter and less hopeless on the return journey but when they reached the back road she suddenly saw something which brought tears to her eyes again. The children from two doors down had built a snowman by their back gate and there he stood with his beady little coal eyes and a carrot for a nose. He made a comical figure but even so Emma dabbed at her eyes with a gloved hand and sniffed loudly.

'Now what's the problem?' said Paul.

'Things keep reminding me of Gamboo.'

Paul raised his eyebrows. 'Even a snowman?'

'Yes, even a snowman. Gamboo once said that one of the things she really missed when she was in Malaya was snow. And I remember saying that we'd make one together this winter; but she never got her snowman after all. I'm not really crying,' Emma said bravely.

'I'm glad about that because I don't think I've got enough energy to take you back there for another shouting session.'

'No, neither have I,' agreed Emma.

Emma went to the funeral on the following day and sat beside her family in their usual pew. It was the first time she'd been in church for a very long time and she felt like a stranger, as though she didn't belong there any more. She'd only come because she loved Gamboo and because today was a time when her parents needed to have family around them. Besides, a funeral was the way people say a last goodbye to those they love . . . and so she must do so too; but it was quite the worst hour and a half of her whole life.

Paul was probably the one who knew most about how she felt and she realised that was why he'd taken her out on the golf course . . . to get her ready to face today. Emma managed to behave in the way she felt was required of her until at last they were back at home and it was all over.

Keeping her outdoor coat on for warmth Emma took the spare key and let herself into the flat. She went from room to room picking things up and then replacing them, trying to remember how she'd felt the last time she'd held that ornament or touched that cushion. The flat wasn't only chilled because the heating had been switched off, it was cold because nobody lived here any more. Going into the bedroom she saw Gamboo's old rocking chair with its red plush seat and backrest and so she sat down and pushed herself backwards and forwards, soothed by the repetitive movement of the creaking rockers.

As she sat there her eyes were drawn to Holman Hunt's painting hanging on the wall opposite Gamboo's bed; she stared at it until her eyes began to close and the rocking chair slowed to a standstill.

Was it her imagination? Was that Gamboo's voice? In those few seconds before sleep takes over it is almost impossible to be sure what you are seeing or hearing.

> . . . Gamboo had just hammered the picture hanger into the wall and was now hanging the painting on it . . . her voice was explaining what the picture meant . . . how the light is always there but if we turn away we can't see it. 'Jesus never forces us to listen,' Gamboo was saying. '. . . He knocks patiently at the door waiting for us to open . . .'

Emma jerked suddenly and opened her eyes. She'd only been asleep for a few moments. Nobody was there . . . there was no voice . . . only the painting still hanging on the wall.

Emma got up from the chair and something made her want to lift the painting down; as she touched it an envelope fell from behind the frame and dropped onto the floor. The envelope was in Gamboo's handwriting and was simply addressed 'To Emma.'

She opened the envelope and took out the letter. From the date she could see that it had been written just before Gamboo first became ill . . . so Emma realised that Gamboo must have known that her illness was coming.

It was quite a long letter but Emma read it over and over again, and as she did so she didn't feel quite so alone any more.

122

My dearest Emma,

By the time you read this letter I shall have gone on the biggest adventure of my life. I am truly looking forward to it so please don't cry, will you. I have an illness which will make great and not very happy changes in me before the end, so I'm writing this while I'm still able.

*But, I want you to remember me as you saw me on that first day we met . . . strong and well and very much alive . . . because **that** is the reality and **that** is the promise that Jesus made to all people. Life abundant is what he said, and that is what I'm going to find when I see him.*

Jesus' love is so great that it is waiting for every living person . . . even those who find it hard to believe.

I can't take any luggage where I'm going so the little painting is yours now.

Love and blessings,

Gamboo

After reading it for the third time Emma put it back carefully in its envelope and then lifted the painting down off the wall; it was Gamboo's last present to her. There was one phrase from the letter which kept going round and round in her mind, '. . . even those who find it hard to believe . . .'

Quite suddenly tears of relief and joy came flooding from her eyes, washing away all trace of hurt and unhappiness. She hadn't wanted to feel like a stranger in church and she hadn't meant to stop believing in Jesus, but once it had happened she couldn't turn back. It was her anger that had forced her away from Jesus but now Gamboo had reminded her that his love was waiting . . . Emma knew that she was safe. Jesus would be her friend again and he must know how sorry she was.

She carried the painting back home and went to find the rest of the family who were sitting in the living room. Mother looked up as she came in.

'We wondered where you'd got to, love.'

Emma propped her painting against the coffee table and was just about to tell them about it when Dad asked, 'Where have you been? You're blue with cold.'

'I've been sitting in Gamboo's bedroom and . . .' but she wasn't given time to finish the sentence.

'Oh, Emma, come here. I know how much you loved Gamboo. We all did, but sitting in that cold flat making yourself miserable isn't going to help.' Mother rubbed Emma's cold hands between her own to warm them.

'Sit at this end nearer the fire,' Paul offered as he shuffled along to the other end of the sofa.

'But I'm not miserable now. That's what I was trying to tell you. I found this behind Gamboo's painting.' She pulled the letter out of her pocket and held it up.

One by one the family read the letter and understood some part of Emma's cheerfulness, but even when she tried to tell them what had happened with the painting and imagining Gamboo's voice they still didn't realise how important it was for Emma.

'What a wonderful letter,' said Dad.

'Gamboo always loved that little painting, didn't she? Are you going to put it in your bedroom?' Mother asked.

'Yes, opposite my bed, like Gamboo had it,' Emma replied.

Much later, when she went upstairs to her room, Emma took down the wild-flower calendar that hung opposite her bed and replaced it with Gamboo's 'Light of the World' painting . . . no, not Gamboo's . . . it was hers now, Emma thought as she looked up at it. She prayed that Jesus would forgive her for turning away and being angry and bitter, then she ended her prayer by asking a blessing on all her family.

Emma opened her eyes. It was such a warm happy feeling to have talked to Jesus again like she'd always done before. She glanced up at her painting hanging there in its new position . . . and then she looked again more closely. Was it only her imagination or had Jesus really smiled at her? Perhaps he had; after all Gamboo had thought she saw him smile.

With that happy thought in her mind Emma snuggled down under the bedclothes and it wasn't long before she gently drifted off to sleep.

When she opened her eyes it was morning. A wintry sun shone in making dappled patterns on the wall, and on the window ledge there was a robin ruffling his cherry red breast feathers and chirping merrily. His chirping soon brought his wife and together they pecked at the crumbs Emma had saved for them off her supper plate.

'I wish I understood bird language,' she said to the two busy little birds.

The female robin looked in through the glass and seemed to be looking straight at Emma; then she began to chirp and sing for several minutes.

'I'll bet you're saying . . . it's good to be alive, wherever you happen to live.'

A sudden feeling that everything was all right and just as it should be swept through Emma's mind. She felt so sure about everything now.

Gamboo wasn't old and frail any more . . . she and Great-Grandad were young and happy living in another sort of world . . . they had loved each other and love lasts for ever. So, what Gamboo had told her about the promise that Jesus had made must be true after all.

'Thank you, Jesus . . . for everything,' Emma said.